"That's Better,"

he murmured in husky approval, his mouth continuing to move over hers.

Wave after wave of sensation flooded her mind beneath his overwhelming onslaught. Her senses were alive to the male strength of his body against the feminine softness of hers.

"No!" she muttered fiercely, fighting her traitorous responses. "I won't let you do this to me." She pushed away with all her strength. "Let me go, Daniel!"

Daniel lifted his head at her last demanding cry and gazed at her in patent disbelief. "You're turning me away, just like that?"

"I am."

SARA CHANCE

is a "wife, mother, author, in that order," who currently resides in Florida with her husband. With the ocean minutes from her front door, Ms. Chance enjoys both swimming and boating.

Dear Reader:

SILHOUETTE DESIRE is an exciting new line of contemporary romances from Silhouette Books. During the past year, many Silhouette readers have written in telling us what other types of stories they'd like to read from Silhouette, and we've kept these comments and suggestions in mind in developing SILHOUETTE DESIRE.

DESIREs feature all of the elements you like to see in a romance, plus a more sensual, provocative story. So if you want to experience all the excitement, passion and joy of falling in love, then SILHOUETTE DESIRE is for you.

I hope you enjoy this book and all the wonderful stories to come from SILHOUETTE DESIRE. I'd appreciate any thoughts you'd like to share with us on new SILHOUETTE DESIRE, and I invite you to write to us at the address below:

Karen Solem
Editor-in-Chief
Silhouette Books
P.O. Box 769
New York, N.Y. 10019

SARA CHANCE
Home At Last

Silhouette Desire
Published by Silhouette Books New York
America's Publisher of Contemporary Romance

Other Silhouette Books by Sara Chance

Her Golden Eyes

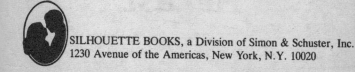

SILHOUETTE BOOKS, a Division of Simon & Schuster, Inc.
1230 Avenue of the Americas, New York, N.Y. 10020

Copyright © 1983 by Sydney Clary

Distributed by Pocket Books

ISBN: 0-671-47527-4

First Silhouette Books printing August, 1983

10 9 8 7 6 5 4 3 2 1

America's Publisher of Contemporary Romance

Printed in the U.S.A.

For David.

To speak without words,
To hear without sound,
To understand without explanation,
This is the love you give to me.

1

"Jenny, here's another Masters' farewell for you," a light female voice announced over the phone.

Jennifer Brown wrinkled her short nose and chuckled at Penny's resigned tone. "Not again?" she groaned in mock surprise. She reached for the ivy- and rose-bordered florist card she knew she would need for the last good-bye of a short-term romance.

"Third blonde this year," Penny confirmed with a laugh.

Cradling the receiver against her shoulder, Jenny rapidly took down Penny's order for the usual elaborate bouquet of yellow roses and the brief message that accompanied them.

"Do you know that he's already got someone to fill Lilly's place!"

Jenny grinned at her high school friend's scandalized tone. Happily married with two kids, Penny couldn't seem to understand her boss's determined pursuit of the ladies.

"So?" Jenny prompted, unable to resist teasing the straitlaced woman a little. She knew Daniel Masters was out of the office, otherwise Penny never would have voiced her thoughts aloud. Normally, she was the epitome of an efficient secretary. She had to be. Daniel Masters wouldn't have tolerated anything else.

Knowing Penny was well into a detailed description of Daniel's latest love interest, Jenny allowed herself the luxury of calling to mind the heir to one of Knoxville's oldest families, Daniel Masters. Golden-haired, blue-eyed, with a lean build perfectly suited to his sophisticated image, he was the man every woman dreamed of in her most vivid fantasies, and Jenny was no exception. Since high school, she had been drawn to the magical aura surrounding Daniel Masters, although not for a young teenager's usual reasons. Daniel represented all that was lacking in Jenny's life: a home, security, a name to be proud of and a place in the world.

What she didn't admire was his preference for gorgeous blondes. She frowned in irritation at her reaction. She should have put away her daydreams long ago, she realized suddenly. Determined to banish his image from her mind, Jenny concentrated on Penny's bubbling chatter.

"—how long this one will last?"

"Look, Penny, I've got to run. Billy's down sick with the flu so I'm doing the deliveries," Jenny interrupted with a quick apology. "I'll see the roses get out by noon."

Jenny hung up the phone, her mind already juggling the endless lists of jobs she had to do before the day was over. It was a good thing Maggie was coming in.

Tucking a pencil into the silky brown topknot perched on top of her head, Jenny stuffed the clip of the flower orders into the oversized pocket of her brilliantly patterned work smock.

The insistent buzz of the back doorbell announced

her assistant's arrival. "Hi, Jen. Gorgeous morning," Maggie bubbled as she breezed in.

"Is it?" Jenny replied skeptically, thinking of the double duty waiting for her. It was on days like this that she wondered why she had bought out old Mrs. Griffin. Being the owner of the small, established florist shop had seemed to represent the embodiment of her dream for belonging. Never having known her parents, or even possessing a name or birthday that was truly hers, Jennifer had longed passionately for a home of her own. She had finally found it in the Garden of Eden.

"What's the problem?" Maggie slipped her amply curved figure into a crisp smock similar to the one her boss wore. Her twinkling blue eyes held a permanent smile of good humor, which usually found an answering response in the young woman she assisted. But not today.

Jenny shrugged, not really certain what was getting her down. "Billy's sick again," she replied, finally voicing her main cause for annoyance.

Maggie's brows rose comically. "Again? Ye gods, that kid sure is something. Wanna bet it's that new little hairdresser at Betty's keeping him out late at night?"

Jenny removed the orders from her pocket and began pinning them to the bulletin board above her work table. "I didn't know he had a new girl," she murmured absently, already reaching for the round bowl she intended to fill with violets for her first delivery.

"I'm not surprised," Maggie commented in a slightly raised voice from the main shop. "I wouldn't have known myself if I hadn't seen them out a few times."

Deftly, Jennie began arranging the delicate purple blossoms she had taken from the refrigeration unit at

9

the rear of the store into an artistic creation. Behind her, she could hear Maggie preparing to open for the day by watering the flowers and plants lining the front window and the display shelves, filling the register and finally flipping the CLOSED sign to OPEN.

Long practice and the three-year association that had begun with Jennifer's purchase of the flower shop made their early morning ritual a smooth operation requiring no direction from Jennifer. That left her free to concentrate on creating her floral offerings and to indulge in the light gossip Maggie so enjoyed.

"Guess who else has a new girl," Jenny commented aloud, entering the display area, her first completed arrangement cradled in her hands. She elbowed open the glass sliding door to the smaller refrigerator recessed into the half wall separating her workroom from the rest of the shop, and placed the vivid cluster on the top rack of the empty case.

"Who?"

Jenny turned around, smiling at the avid interest in Maggie's voice. Although she had to be sixty if she were a day, the older woman was remarkably childlike in her curiosity about other people. Widowed and childless after nearly forty-two years of happy marriage, she had appeared on the doorstep one morning soon after Jennifer took over the store and applied for a job. Jenny had hired her on the spot, never once regretting her decision. She had become a friend, her romantic personality a perfect foil for Jennifer's more realistic, practical nature.

"Daniel Masters," Jenny drawled slowly, ignoring the slight pang his name brought. She would get over her teenage crush if it killed her, she vowed.

"He got rid of Lilly *already?*" Maggie squeaked. "It hasn't even been two months. That's short even for him." She shook her head, the silver white curls framing her face bouncing gently with the force of her movement. "Poor man. He has the worst luck with women."

"Poor man?" Jenny echoed in astonishment, all amusement fading at Maggie's incredible observation. "Are you kidding? That man has everything anyone could want. Azalea Hill has got to be *the* most beautiful home in all of Tennessee. And he has more money than he could possibly spend in fifty lifetimes, not to mention a family the whole community respects."

The twinkle in Maggie's eyes dimmed at Jenny's scathing summation. "He hasn't got love, honey," she stated with beautiful simplicity.

Jenny snorted, drawing herself up to her full five feet seven inches. Anger at Daniel for his free life-style and herself for caring made her normally soft voice sharp. "Love? He doesn't know the meaning of the word. Why, he goes through women like a fox in the henyard."

Maggie giggled at the country expression, then sobered. "Sure he does. He's looking for someone to care about," she retorted seriously.

The utter sincerity in the other woman's tone completely silenced Jenny for a moment. She stared at Maggie's wrinkled face, reading the absolute certainty of her belief.

"I suppose next you'll tell me you believe in Santa Claus," Jenny commented finally.

"Everybody has to have faith in something, honey —even you," Maggie murmured, her voice gentle with sympathetic understanding.

"I believe in myself, Maggie," Jennie answered slowly, searching for the words to make Maggie understand. "All my life I've been alone, and I've learned to depend on me for what I want and what I need. The orphanage tried to be a home for me, but it never was." She grimaced ruefully, admitting her own culpability in its failure. "Even some of my foster parents tried, in their own way."

Jennifer's large eyes darkened to slate with the long-buried pain of the barren years of her childhood, the endless stream of state homes for the gangly, unattractive orphan she had been. Later, when she had reached her teenage years, there hadn't even been a boyfriend to alleviate the stark loneliness of her existence. Not that she blamed them. She had been a mousy-haired, freckled creature in hand-me-down dresses with no style at all. Painfully insecure, she had hidden behind a mask of prickliness that repelled rather than attracted.

Maturity had smoothed the rough edges of her personality and dispelled forever the gangly, coltish young body. Slender, graceful limbs replaced the knobby knees, the freckles were now a sprinkle of gold dust across the short, straight nose and lovely, molded cheekbones. Jennifer's best features were her huge, slanted gray eyes fringed with extravagant sable lashes. Not a conventionally pretty face by any means, but one that echoed the character and personality of its owner. Her skin had the soft coloring of a gently faded Regency cameo and the almost translucent quality of fine porcelain. Her mouth was a passionate curve of full lips, which more often than not wore a smile, showing even white teeth.

"Don't look back, child," Maggie scolded gently, interrupting her friend's unhappy memories. "It's what you are now that counts. Look what you've done with only a high school diploma. You bought and made a success of this shop—no mean feat for one of your young years."

"Twenty-seven isn't exactly a spring chicken,"

Jenny disagreed with a hint of a smile to lighten her dark mood. "Besides, I never could have done it if Mrs. Griffin hadn't been so kind about financing me. The banks wouldn't."

Maggie nodded her head at Jennifer's bald assessment. "Not then, no. Most twenty-four-year-olds don't have the determination to succeed that you did."

"Or the reason," Jenny finished cryptically. The cheerful tingle of the silver bell above the front door announced the arrival of their first customer of the day.

"Speaking of succeeding, we'd both better get busy or my final mortgage payment to Bessie will be very late."

"No way, honey. This place was meant to be yours," Maggie denied with a reassuring chuckle as she headed for the lady standing at the potted plant display near the door.

The rest of the morning passed in a blur of activity for Jennifer. It seemed everyone in Knoxville was intent on announcing the end of winter with colorful blossoms of spring. Between the constant jingle of the front bell, the ping of the cash register and the phone, Maggie had been kept running.

Normally, Jennifer would have gone out to help her, but this morning she had enough work to keep two people busy, plus the added headache of the deliveries. It was after eleven when she finally whipped off her smock and hung it up. She had just finished loading the van.

She stuck her head through the connecting door. "I'm going now, Maggie."

Maggie looked up from the young mother she was serving, to nod her agreement. "How long will you be?"

Jenny glanced at the serviceable watch on her

slender wrist. "Two hours should do it. You can have lunch when I get back."

"I might just last that long without wasting away," the amply padded Maggie teased with a good-natured grin.

Jenny was still chuckling when she climbed into her light green truck with its distinctive logo of an ivy and rose border. She quickly scanned the list of stops on the clipboard attached to the dash. The shortage of time remaining before noon dictated Lilly's Deane Hill Drive address had to be her first stop. As she joined the heavy midday traffic on Kingston Pike, the shortest and quickest way to her destination, she wondered what Daniel Masters' next girlfriend looked like. Probably blond, stacked and sexy, she decided cynically, recalling Billy's graphic descriptions of his last two women and knowing firsthand the voluptuous statistics of his soon-to-be ex, Lilly Tyler. What was his fascination with the bombshell type? It was an open secret that Edna Masters wanted her son to marry.

Mentally berating herself for once again allowing her thoughts to stray into forbidden territory, Jenny forced her attention back to her driving. She made a left turn up the inclined drive of the posh townhouse complex where Lilly lived, admiring the rolling court-yard beneath the newly budding oak trees as she passed. She parked the van in one of the visitor's slots and got out, sweeping the spring-touched grass and brilliant first blossoms of the seasonal flowers in the center green with an appreciative eye.

It was almost time for the annual Dogwood Arts Festival, when the whole town celebrated the end of winter. There would be art and crafts exhibits, lectures and any number of other cultural events. Best of all, from her point of view, was the beautiful dogwood trail that led through the most picturesque of the Knoxville residential area. The vivid displays of bright yellow daffodils, purple irises, crocuses, and tulips, as well as the distinctive flowering dogwood trees, made it a sight to gladden the heart of any plant lover.

Balancing the rose bouquet in one hand, Jennifer pushed the doorbell to Lilly's townhouse. The scent of the blossoms teased her nose as she waited.

This was her favorite time of the year. The rebirth, the renewal of life from winter's barren soil seemed to symbolize her own empty childhood and the spring she had worked so hard for.

"Yes?" The husky southern drawl interrupted Jennifer's thoughts.

Startled, she glanced up, seeing a negligee-clad blonde standing in the now open doorway. "Garden of Eden Florists," Jenny explained with a professional smile. Even without the name on the order, she would have recognized Lilly Tyler, one of the town's favorite entertainers.

The woman returned her greeting, then held the door open invitingly. "C'mon in, sugah." She waved her slender, pale hands expressively, sending a waft of expensive nail polish in Jenny's direction. "Would you put them on the table for me? I'm afraid my nails are still wet."

Obeying, Jenny placed the tall vase on the small glass and chrome hall stand just inside the door and turned to go.

"Oo, I wonder who they're from? I just love roses, don't you?" the woman gushed, leaning over to inhale the delicious scent of the golden blossoms.

Jenny smiled politely, edging carefully for the door. She didn't want to be around when this one read Masters' brief farewell note. Applauded in her own sphere and artistically temperamental, Lilly was fully capable of causing a scene.

"Would you open the card for me?" Lilly wiggled her fingers as though emphasizing the reason for her request.

Jenny hesitated, unable to think of a single excuse for refusing. Deftly she removed the small green envelope from the pronged plastic stick anchored in the center of the flowers and opened it. Passing the ivy- and rose-bordered card to Lilly, Jenny watched as she quickly scanned the short message. Having written the note, Jenny had no difficulty recalling the wording:

> My dear Lilly,
>   May these golden roses symbolize the memorable times we had together.
>
> > Your most devoted fan,
> > Daniel

The excitement faded from Lilly's face while she read. Her eyes narrowed in anger. "That stinkin' rat!" Lilly exclaimed with a sharp edge to her slow drawl. "I'll fix his red wagon! Just wait!"

Unwilling amusement twinkled in Jenny's eyes as she saw Lilly take a deep breath, swelling her amply endowed bosom in the fragile bodice of her pink negligee. She wondered which would give first: the seams, or Lilly's control. Fortunately, her composure held, and so did her gown. Jenny had to admire her restraint. The singer's anger was an almost tangible force in the air.

"I suppose you have delivered these little bunches," she flicked a derisive finger at one yellow blossom, "a dozen times before," Lilly commented bitterly.

"Not dozens, no," Jenny denied quietly.

Lilly stared at her, a thoughtful frown on her face,

replacing some of her anger. "You're not the regular delivery person, are you?"

Jenny shook her head, wondering what was coming next. "He's sick today," she explained briefly.

The blonde moved smoothly toward the door, only her rigid carriage betraying the emotion locked inside her. "I won't keep you then."

"Well, how did it go?" Maggie asked as Jenny entered the back door of the shop nearly thirty minutes later than she had anticipated.

Hanging the van's key on the hook above the work table, Jenny wrinkled her nose expressively. "Rotten, if you must know." She leaned against the table with a tired sigh. "I nearly got bitten by a German shepherd at my last stop."

Maggie chuckled. "I never knew Billy's job was so hazardous."

"Neither did I," Jenny agreed with feeling.

Maggie walked over to the small bar-sized refrigerator and pulled out a covered plastic container. "Was the traffic that bad?" she asked curiously. She gestured to the carton she held. "Want to share my tuna salad, or did you stop somewhere on the way back?"

Jenny shook her head. "I brought some cheese and crackers and a thermos of lime freezes—enough to share," she offered, knowing how much Maggie liked the lemon-lime soda blended with crushed ice and lime sherbet.

Maggie made no secret of her pleasure as she quickly set out the paper plates and disposable glasses on the small table by the refrigerator. "Let's just hope no one comes in so we can eat in peace."

Jenny looked up from filling their glasses with the frothy green liquid. "Bite you tongue, lady. I'm in business to make money," she rebuked half seriously.

Maggie heaped her plate with a generous portion of salad and cheddar cheese. "I know. Tough businesswoman who'll do just about anything for money," she agreed waving her fork for emphasis. "Pooh!"

Tipping her head to one side, Jenny studied her friend. Her expression lost some of its lightness. "You're right, in a way. Money itself isn't really what I work for." She paused, her own lunch forgotten for a moment. "I want to be someone. Not famous or anything. Just an ordinary person who has made something of her life."

Maggie reached across the table to pat her hand. "You are that already, child."

"No, not yet. One day when I have a family of my own, maybe." Embarrassment tinged Jenny's cheeks. She laughed self-consciously at the sudden revelation of her deepest desires.

Maggie nodded in sage agreement. "If anyone should have a home and kids, it's you. I swear you must be the Pied Piper of east Tennessee," Maggie chuckled. "Are you going to help coach the girls' swim team this year?"

"Probably," Jenny murmured between bites. "Unless this new coach already has his assistant lined up."

"I'll bet he doesn't. Not many people have the time or will make it to lend a hand with problem kids," Maggie argued.

Jennifer shifted in her seat, as usual extremely ill at ease in the face of praise. "I don't have many commitments," she explained dismissively.

Maggie's raised brows showed her opinion of this blatant falsehood. She left unsaid the reminder of Jenny's six-day-a-week business, the two-bedroom apartment she kept alone or the numerous parties and charity affairs she catered florally.

"Besides, I distinctly recall at the end-of-the-year picnic a certain someone who planned and cooked the lion's share," Jenny retaliated, watching with amusement the color rising in Maggie's parchment cheeks.

"I wasn't doing anything else." Maggie's automatic defense trailed away at the knowing look in Jennifer's shrewd eyes.

Taking pity on her friend, Jenny ceased her teasing. She stood up, gathering her empty dishes together. "Looks like for once we got to eat without any interruptions."

Seizing the change of subject gratefully, Maggie agreed. "I'll bet it doesn't last."

"I hope not!" Jennifer went over to her work table and climbed onto her stool before studying the order list. "Remember the mortgage."

"The Garden of Eden's battle cry," Maggie shot back before she headed for the store area.

The afternoon was a repeat of the hectic morning, with the notable exception of the hungry German shepherd and Daniel Masters' volatile ex-girlfriend. Jennifer finally locked up nearly two hours later than usual. With a tired sigh, she mounted the back stairs, which led to her apartment over the shop. The disadvantages in living above her business paled next to the convenience of being only twenty-two steps away from her own front entrance at the end of a long day like this one.

As she opened her door, the familiar scent of the potpourri in tiny copper pots about her apartment assailed her senses. The haunting fragrance spelled home to Jenny's weary body. She kicked off her shoes, her aching feet sinking into the fur of the rich cinnamon shag carpet. She wriggled her toes appre-

ciatively before padding across the comfortably fur-
nished peach- and lime-toned living room to the
kitchen. She took a peek in the oven at the homemade chicken potpie that was bubbling gently beneath its golden pastry crust. Her dinner, like the
lights and the heat, was set on an automatic timer
that allowed her to come home after a hard day to a
warm welcome and a hot meal. It wasn't as good as
a family of her own, but it was better than the cold,
stark darkness it could have been.

To dispel the quiet, Jennifer switched on her
stereo, and immediately the raspy, deep-throated
growl of Kenny Rogers filled the air. Humming
along, Jenny set the small oak table in the dining
alcove with a peach gingham place mat and white
china. As she sat down to eat, her eyes roamed over
the place she had created for herself. It had been a
drab rental when she had first bought the shop
building from Bessie Griffin.

Taking her favorite colors as her main decorating
theme, she had stripped the dark papered walls and
painted them a soft white. The furniture, most of it
from secondhand stores, was one-of-a-kind, sturdy
pieces she had chosen with an eye for style and
refinished with loving patience until the old wood
was beautifully restored. The long, luxuriously
stuffed couch was one of her more adventurous
finds. With Maggie's expert help, she had removed
the original sickly green velvet and replaced it with a
delicate peach floral cotton. Small individually fashioned throw pillows of lemon and lime were scattered haphazardly in the sofa corners and also in the
two wingback chairs that composed the grouping.
Her bedroom and adjoining bath echoed her color
scheme with pale green walls and peach velvet
bedspread, drapes and towels. The extra bedroom
was turned into her workman's study, where utility

combined with beauty was the key. It was a home that catered to the total person—a haven of aesthetic pleasure, inviting relaxation and peace.

It was a giant step up for the nameless orphan educated by the state. Heaven alone knew what or who her people had been. In her idealistic youth, when she still believed in miracles, she felt that someday she would find the answers to her blind heritage. Yet as the years passed, the need to know had faded in importance. Building a life for herself was an all-consuming task. She had no advantages to start with. Each step had to be planned carefully and then worked for. Her barren background offered no support. Her single-minded determination had left her little time for the usual romantic relationships. It was only recently that she had dated at all.

Jennifer slid into bed marveling at the absence of the bitterness she had once known for her desertion. That early parental abandonment now produced only one unshakable emotion in her: a determination never to repeat the mistake of the woman who gave birth to her. She would *never, ever* risk bringing an unwanted child into the world. She smiled, remembering the shock of her latest attractive escort when she had refused to share his bed. Straitlaced prude, he had called her.

Jenny grinned at the memory of his thwarted attempts to seduce her. It was amazing what an elbow in the right place could do. A younger Jenny might have been hurt by his accusations, but not this Jenny. Somehow she had never questioned her ability to respond to a man. It didn't matter that so far none of her dates had raised more than the mildest feelings in her. When the time was right . . .

Just before Jenny drifted off, Daniel Masters' handsome face imposed itself on her mind. Now there was a man who wouldn't resort to ugly taunts when his lovemaking attempts failed. Thinking of Daniel brought to mind Lilly Tyler and her angry promise of retribution. Fleetingly, a vision of an upended vase of yellow roses over a certain sleek male head floated through her sleepy mind.

"Poor Daniel," she murmured, unconsciously echoing Maggie's earlier observation. "You may not have love, but you sure have Lilly." Sleep claimed Jenny before she could finish her provocative thought.

2

The next morning, Jenny entered her workroom, pausing only long enough to slip into her smock before going into the main shop. This was the day she normally gave to changing her front window display. Keeping in mind the season, she had decided to do a colorful woodland scene featuring Peter Cottontail and all his friends. She removed the backdrop from the previous presentation of a snow-covered glen where the impudent heads of bright yellow daffodils and purple irises emerged from scattered nooks, depicting the approaching spring. Overhead, a dogwood tree, its bare branches sprinkled in white, showed the promise of green to come.

Working quickly, she stripped the fluffy cotton froth from the snow-blanketed floor and the lovely small potted Norfolk pines that surrounded the miniature winter scene where a couple snuggled cozily beneath a fur rug in a small, horse-drawn sleigh. Engrossed in her work, Jenny didn't respond immediately to the insistent tapping on the shop's window.

Finally the sound penetrated her absorption,

drawing her attention. She stared at the tall blonde gesturing impatiently at the front door.

Shaking her head, Jenny pointed to the 9:00 A.M. opening posted in plain view on the OPEN/CLOSED sign.

The woman held up a bulging grocery bag and repeated her hand signals. Sighing in resignation, Jenny stepped down from the window.

"I wonder what Lilly Tyler wants?" she muttered under her breath as she unlocked the door. Pinning a polite smile on her face, she studied her visitor.

"You're the woman who came yesterday. Good! May I see you for a moment. I know you aren't open." Lilly paused in her running monologue long enough to take a breath and let Jenny get a word in.

"I don't mean to be rude, but—" Jenny began, only to be interrupted.

"It's important."

Shrugging helplessly, Jenny moved aside, allowing Lilly to sweep past her, trailing a wake of exotic perfume. Jenny followed her to the cash counter, where Lilly deposited her bag with a thud.

"I would like you to make up a very special order for me. It must be delivered at 11:15 sharp," she explained briefly, all evidence of the soft drawl of the day before wiped away by an anger scarcely controlled. "Do it and you can name your own price."

"What did you have in mind?" Jennifer questioned warily, not liking the vengeful expression on the blonde's expertly made up face.

"This." Lilly carefully upended her sack, spilling out a collection of stinkweed, sneeze weeds, thistles and nettles, a length of tatty burlap and one battered china basin with a handle.

"Is that what I think it is?" Jennifer asked, fingering the cracked brown pottery.

Lilly nodded, a thin smile curving her lips. "A chamber pot."

Suddenly Jennifer realized what the other woman intended to do. The knowledge brought a frown to her face as she studied first the motley assortment of weeds and then the angry ex-girlfriend.

"I want you to fix this stuff into an arrangement for me and I want it delivered personally to Daniel Masters in his board meeting at 11:15," Lilly ordered grimly. "If I thought I'd get by that secretary of his, I'd do it myself just to see his face, the stinkin' rat!"

A smile tugged at Jennifer's lips, imagining the polished Daniel Masters, pillar of the community, receiving his own little farewell bouquet from his latest bedmate. "Where on earth did you come up with such an idea?"

Lilly's face reflected her annoyance at Jennifer's reaction. "I don't see what's so funny," she mumbled, the beginnings of a grin tugging at her compressed lips. "I had to get up at dawn and trudge over at least six cow fields to gather this mess. Just look at my shoes." She pointed to the dainty spectator heels now liberally coated with mud and whatever.

Lilly's indignation, plus the image of Daniel's reception of his lady love's token, sent Jenny into peals of mirth that brought tears to her eyes.

Within seconds, both women were leaning against the counter, the scattered roadside posies between them, giggling like schoolgirls.

"It's priceless," Jenny pronounced on a stifled chuckle. "But I can't do it," she added on a more sober note.

Instantly Lilly's amusement died. "Why not?" she asked in honest bewilderment.

Jenny gestured expressively toward her shop.

"Because I like my business too much to let anything jeopardize it. I've worked hard to get where I am. Daniel Masters is a good customer and—"

"I'll bet," Lilly interrupted tartly. "I received a few bouquets from this place in my reign. As a woman, you must have some feelings about the behavior of a man like Daniel?"

Jennifer shrugged, not liking the blonde's pointed attack. "It's not up to me to judge his relationships one way or the other. From all I hear, his women are beautiful, sophisticated, and well able to take care of themselves," Jennifer stated bluntly. She eyed her visitor, daring her to deny her assessment.

Lilly's gaze was the first to drop. "Then you won't do it," she stated with obvious disappointment.

Jenny hesitated, her refusal dying on her lips. Lilly did have a valid point. She *was* tired of seeing Daniel send his women packing with *her* flowers. By his own hand, she was involved with his romantic escapades, even if indirectly. It bothered her, and suddenly she couldn't control the urge to do something about it. It would be nice to turn the tables on him for once. But how to do it without risking her business reputation? She stared off into space, lost in thought. She missed the curiosity on Lilly's face as she waited silently for her to speak.

Coming to a decision, Jennifer faced Lilly squarely. "I'll do it on two conditions," she announced finally. "First, there will be no public humiliation of the man. Two, Garden of Eden is not connected with this in any way, either by payment or word. This is just between the two of us."

"Okay," Lilly responded quickly. "When will he get it?"

"As soon as possible." Jennifer felt the first twinge of regret at her impulsive offer when she glimpsed the triumphant satisfaction in the blonde's eyes.

"Now I must ask you to leave. I've got a lot to do if I'm to get this done today."

Having gained her objective, Lilly smiled and headed obediently for the door. She paused for a second to dig in her handbag. She pulled out a small, mud-brown envelope and pressed it into Jenny's hands. "This goes with it, please?"

Jenny stared at the sealed square, then doubtfully back at Lilly's defiant face.

"I just told him what I thought of his tactics. Nothing else, I promise," she explained hurriedly, reading the indecision in Jennifer's expression.

Reluctantly pocketing the note, Jennifer unlocked the door. "Just remember our agreement," she warned in farewell.

Lilly's "I will" rang in her ears as she turned back to her weed-strewn counter. The earthenware pot sat in majestic splendor among the stems and flowers. Jennifer fingered the tiny blossoms of the wild greenery, suddenly appreciating their untamed appeal. An idea bloomed. Lilly's gesture *was* funny, but it didn't need to be the tatty creation the singer obviously envisioned. With a little imagination, it could be very attractive.

She checked the time, thanking the powers that be that she had come in so early. With any luck, Penny would be in her office and she could deliver Lilly's little offering before Masters arrived.

Cradling the phone on her shoulder, Jenny quickly dialed her friend. While she waited for her to answer, she deftly began arranging the weeds in the chamber pot, using the supplies Maggie kept under her counter.

When Penny's voice bubbled a cheerful "Good morning" in her ear, she didn't pause in her task.

"When is your boss due in today?" she began without preamble.

"About 9:30 or 10. Why?" Penny asked curiously.

"Good," Jenny muttered, fixing the last nettle into place.

"What's wrong, Jen? You don't sound right."

"I'm fine, Penny. I just have a delivery for Mr. Masters. Today is going to be busy so I was hoping to bring it over now."

"Okay, we can probably manage coffee together if you hurry," Penny agreed, happily oblivious to Jenny's barely concealed reluctance to go.

"I'll hurry, all right," Jenny mumbled after she hung up. With a couple of knots and some judicious clippng with her scissors, she fashioned a wide bow from the tattered burlap.

Stepping back, she observed the finished product. Not a beautiful floral piece, yet it did have a rustic charm. The tiny multihued blossoms sprinkled among the spiky greenery somehow complemented the rough textured burlap and the cracked pottery. But nothing could disguise the chamber pot, Jenny decided glumly. She had to be out of her mind to agree to this.

"A rose is a rose and a chamber pot is still a portable toilet," she misquoted as she searched under the register for a box to cover her creation. At least there was no chance of seeing the recipient face to face, she reminded herself. It was a coward's way out—that she had no hesitation in using.

Collecting her box with its attached note, Jenny climbed into the van. She blessed the early hour for the relatively quiet streets that allowed her to reach the Masters complex in record time. Her tennis shoes made little sound as she entered the delivery entrance of the four-storied office building and headed for the upper floor.

The elevator whisked her nonstop to the very heart of Masters' territory. The doors slid open noiselessly, revealing the opulent yet functional reception area. Normally, Jenny would have paused here and given her name to the girl on duty. But the sleek, modern desk was vacant. Sheer habit from the times she had picked up Penny for lunch made Jenny hesitate for a split second before passing through the long corridor branching off to her right. At the end of the hall, huge carved double doors guarded Daniel Masters' inner sanctum.

Shifting the box she carried to a precarious one-handed grip—the darned thing seemed to be gaining an ounce with every step she took—Jenny knocked briefly, then opened the door.

Penny looked up from the file spread on the desk in front of her with a smile. "That was quick. You must have flown."

Smiling slightly, Jenny walked toward her. "Not nearly fast enough, believe me," she commented in heartfelt tones.

Penny's eyebrow rose in startled inquiry. "What on earth do you mean, and what's in the box?" she questioned all in one breath.

Jenny carefully placed the anonymous white square box on the corner of Penny's desk before raising deceptively innocent eyes to her friend's face. "Would you believe, *flowers* for your boss?" The faint emphasis placed on the contents drew a puzzled look.

"Why are they covered up, Jen? Can I open it?" Penny barely waited for Jenny's nod before untying the string around the box. Her expression mirrored her excited curiosity over the unusual gift.

Jenny watched her face change dramatically as she pushed back the concealing green tissue to reveal the tiny colored flowers and prickly greenery of the weeds. Penny reached in and slowly lifted the arrangement from its cushioned nest.

"What is this . . . ?" her voice trailed away as she recognized the distinctive shape she held. "Oh my goodness!" There was a wealth of horrified amazement in the slow, shocked drawl. Penny stared at Jenny. "Who?" she mouthed blankly.

Jenny couldn't help it. The appalled expression on Penny's face was too much. The amusement that had lingered since Lilly had dumped her bag on her counter surfaced. She grinned impishly, "Can't you guess?" She glanced significantly to the card displayed prominently on the box lid.

"Lilly!"

"Lilly." Jenny agreed with a chuckle.

Penny twisted the pottery from side to side, her stunned expression giving way to comprehension as she recognized the stinkweed and sneezeweed among the thistles and nettles. Suddenly she was giggling like a teenager.

"He'll wring her neck, but it's perfect, just perfect. Only she would have the nerve to pull something like this."

Jenny grabbed for the pot as Penny began laughing uproariously.

"Wait until the boss sees it," Penny gasped, retaining her grip on the pot.

"Wait until I see what?" a deep, southern voice echoed from the open doorway.

Startled, both women whirled as one, barely retaining their dual hold on Lilly's gift. Penny's surprised "Oh, no!" masked Jenny's indrawn breath of dismay. She saw the beginnings of an attractive smile die when he realized what they had in their hands.

Jenny shut her eyes briefly, praying for a tornado, anything to swoop down and bodily remove her from the path of Daniel Masters. Beside her, she heard Penny gulp nervously.

She lifted her lashes slowly as Penny, with all the instincts of an intelligent coward, released her hold on the chamber pot. With an apologetic glance at Jennifer's frozen figure, she grabbed up the file on her desk. "I was just on my way to the copy machine," she mumbled hurriedly before fleeing the room.

Daniel Masters watched her go, an expression of sardonic amusement on his handsome face.

With his attention diverted for a moment, Jenny edged cautiously for the invitingly open doorway. In her haste to escape, she forgot she still held the weeds.

Daniel's quiet spoken command reminded her, "Not so fast, Miss whoever-you-are."

Jenny halted abruptly, finding her path blocked by Daniel's tall form. She stared at him blankly, her eyes wide. He towered over her, this golden-haired aristocrat. The arrogance of command and years of fine breeding lay in the tilt of his head and the easy way he dominated the room . . . and Jenny. She couldn't remember the last time a man or his looks stopped her cold in her tracks. It wasn't a good feeling, she discovered.

Lean, sleek, with a rich tan that no sunlamp ever produced, he was a fine-tempered sword poised for battle and she was the target. The stunningly blue eyes beneath winged, tawny brows were twin daggers to her mesmerized eyes.

Unable to move, she watched as he took a step forward, bringing him close enough to lift the burden from her hands. Daniel studied the arrangement silently, his face an unreadable mask. Finally he lowered it carefully to the corner of the desk.

Jenny knew then she regretted her part in this prank more than she thought possible. What had seemed nothing more than a harmless tilt at this man's amorous way of life now took on a new dimension. She saw her own actions with new eyes, and didn't like her image. Suddenly her part in the joke seemed mean and petty. It didn't help her conscience a bit to know it wasn't what she had intended. She had the oddest sensation he was somehow hurt by Lilly's gesture. The anger she had expected was there; but under it, was there a glimpse of something else?

"I suppose there is a card to go with this little . . . gift?" The silky question was velvet over steel that demanded an answer.

"On the box lid," Jenny murmured, grateful her voice worked even if her legs didn't. She just managed to avoid shrinking away when Daniel, without shifting his position, reached around her and removed the brown envelope.

With a cursory look at the distinctive handwriting, he tossed the note back on the lid. "Very appropriate," he commented, his eyes openly raking Jenny's jean-clad form before coming to rest on her face. "Where do you come in?"

Jennifer moistened suddenly dry lips with the tip of her tongue before drawing a controlled deep breath and letting it out slowly. Anger at herself for allowing Daniel's physical presence to overpower her sparked in her eyes. "I'm just the delivery person," she stated with measured composure. "Now that I've done my job, I'll be on my way." She edged sideways to go around him.

Daniel's hand on her arm stopped her. "Does the delivery person have a name?"

Jennifer's eyes fastened incredulously on the slender fingers holding her immobile before her gaze flew to his face. She sensed his restraint even without the telltale clenched jaw. Seeing the determination reflected there, she shrugged. "Jennifer."

The tawny head nodded slowly, the crystal blue eyes never leaving hers. "Did you know what was in the box?"

Jenny's lashes flickered slightly, giving him the answer he sought.

The hand on her arm dropped away as though it had been scorched.

"Why did you do it? I don't even know you," he muttered. His eyes reflected a mixture of puzzlement and anger.

Jenny shook her head. She couldn't shake the feeling that he was hurt by Lilly's gesture. It was an absurd notion that denied logic. Was it possible he didn't realize how cool his good-byes seemed to his women? She wished more than ever that she could leave. Sympathy stirred within her, a need to mitigate some of the pain that Lilly, with her help, had inflicted. To irritate him and perhaps, make him rethink his seemingly cavalier treatment of her sex was one thing. But this . . . this somehow wasn't funny. Honesty demanded she give him the truth.

"I know Lilly," she explained slowly, choosing her words with care. "She was upset by your change toward her and took this way to relieve her feelings. I agreed to deliver it." She paused, meeting his intense gaze bravely. "Now I wish I hadn't."

"I always believed she understood," he murmured, obviously speaking his thoughts aloud. "It never occurred to me she would feel so strongly when it was time for us to part. Damn it, she knows the rules!"

For the first time since Daniel appeared, Jenny smiled with some amusement. "She knew the rules so well, she rose at dawn and tramped around the soggy countryside looking for the 'flowers' she needed for her bouquet."

Daniel stared at her in silence for a moment before

the image of the late-night singer up with the sun brought a glimmer of answering laughter to his eyes.

"I doubt that she enjoyed that," he agreed solemnly.

"I know she didn't like what the rain last night did to the ground. She had enough mud on her high heels to sink a small boat," Jenny said with a smile, pleased that her small attempt to lighten his mood had succeeded. Her eyes widened in surprise as Daniel's handsome face split in a boyish grin.

"She didn't go out in those spindly little things she usually wears, did she?" he demanded.

The vivid picture of Lilly's mud-spattered nylons and navy heels saved her from admitting she hadn't noticed what Lilly normally wore. There was an imperceptible hesitation before Jenny nodded.

"It's a wonder she didn't twist an ankle or break a leg. And all to get back at me!" Daniel commented, both puzzled and amused.

Seizing the mercurial mood change gratefully, Jenny made a definite move toward the door. "I really must go. I'll be late to work if I don't hurry."

Surprisingly, Daniel made no effort to stop her.

Jenny paused at the threshold to glance back at him. She found him watching her intently, an arrested expression on his face. She wondered at her own reluctance to escape now that she could. "Well . . . good-bye," she offered awkwardly, mentally kicking herself for stopping. She turned away quickly.

"What's your last name?" Daniel's deep-throated question reached out to hold her though she didn't face him.

"Brown," she supplied without thinking.

"Good-bye, Jenny Brown."

The soft farewell echoed in Jennifer's mind all the way back to the shop. For a moment the usually buried romantic side of her emerged, bringing with it the full force of her schoolgirl crush. Was there a tinge of regret in his drawling voice? she wondered. For a split second she savored her fantasy, then reality took over. Daydreamer! she chided herself angrily as she parked her van behind the shop. She was going to put Daniel Masters out of her mind!

"Where in heaven's name have you been, child! Do you realize it's almost nine? The window is half draped. What happened?" Maggie scolded nonstop as Jenny hurried through the shop to the display area.

"I'll tell you all about it later, Maggie," Jenny explained when her assistant had finally allowed her a word. She stepped into the raised platform and began dismantling the rest of the winter scene. She carefully passed the props into Maggie's waiting hands as she worked.

"Did that shipment of roses arrive while I was gone?" Jenny asked. Her mind turned once again to business, completely banishing the devastatingly handsome Daniel Masters to the rarefied air of the outer regions where he belonged.

Maggie nodded without pausing in her task of packing away the things Jenny gave her. "He also left some gorgeous lavender-dyed carnations," Maggie added enthusiastically.

Jenny grinned at the mention of the older woman's favorite color. "I'll bet the flowers didn't enthrall you half as much as the color did. They could've been weeds so long as they were purple." A frown crossed her brow at the reminder of her early-hour delivery. Luckily, Maggie was bent over a storage box with her back to Jenny. She wasn't quite sure how much she wanted to impart of her morning's activities.

Maggie straightened with a mock groan of relief. "I can't help it if you have no taste," she retaliated amicably. The color battle was a long-running feud between them. "I keep telling you to try on a nice shade of lavender, but you won't listen. With that creamy skin of yours and that silky hair, I know you'd be a knockout, especially with those eyes. Lord, I wish I looked like you when I was young. I'd have had every man chasing after me or my name isn't Maggie Simmons."

"You weren't Maggie Simmons then," Jenny shot back, her hands moving deftly among the pots of vivid crocuses and tulips Maggie had so helpfully assembled beside the backdrop.

"So what? You know what I mean." Maggie pushed a three-foot-high yellow bunny into the window area. "At least I wouldn't have spent my time at home alone night after night."

Jenny arranged Peter Cottontail next to the blue foil pond she had rolled out on the floor. She slanted a quick look at Maggie's suddenly serious face. "Since when have you been worrying about my love life?" She pointed to the large colorful Easter basket on the stone tile at Maggie's feet. "I'm ready for that."

Bending to retrieve the holiday container, Maggie didn't answer immediately. She waited until Jennifer met her eyes.

"Someone has to. It's a sure bet you aren't going to," she stated forthrightly. "Why, look at the way you sent Jim Nichols about his business. Why, I could . . . I don't know what!" She shook her head in exasperated disgust. "You're young. You ought to be out doing things."

Sheer surprise held Jennifer motionless. She hadn't realized Maggie's concern. She had thought her friend understood her driving need for a home of her own and security. "This is a great time to be delving into my romantic life," she teased with a grin, seeking to lighten the atmosphere between them. "We open in ten minutes, you know."

"Oh, yes, the shop comes first." Maggie's voice held a note of irritation Jennifer had never heard before—at least not aimed at her. She bent, gathered the remaining stuffed woodland creatures in her arms and thrust them at Jennifer. "When are you planning on fitting a man in your life?" Maggie's plump, rosy cheeks ballooned as she bit off her words.

Jennifer carefully arranged her furry animals among the gay blooming crocuses, irises, daffodils and lilies before replying. "I don't know what you're so het up about, Maggie," she commented as she worked.

"I know you don't. That's what makes it so damned unbelievable," Maggie cried.

Jennifer's head shot up at her friend's uncharacteristic use of a swear word. Her gray eyes held a questioning appeal when she stared into Maggie's annoyed face. The vivid miniature Easter glen she was creating was forgotten. "What have I done, Maggie?" she asked softly. "Is it so terrible to want a place that is truly mine? To be someone?"

"You can't run your life like you run this shop. Love doesn't wait for the right time between the right people. It's a wild, beautiful, living thing. You can't put love in a cubbyhole with no fertilizer or sunlight and expect it to survive." Maggie's eloquent appeal was obviously deeply felt.

"I don't think I'm doing that," Jenny protested.

"Yes you are, child. Open your eyes before it's too late. You're twenty-seven now and you don't even have a steady beau."

Avoiding Maggie's perceptive gaze, Jenny stared at the display at her feet, a fine flush of embarrassment tinting her skin a soft pink. "The last 'beau,' as you call him, wanted bed with no marriage. I can't do that." She raised silver gray eyes in a plea for understanding. "You know why."

Maggie nodded. "I do, but that shouldn't stop you from looking. Somewhere out there a man is waiting for you. Maybe you've already met him."

Instantly Daniel Masters' image invaded Jenny's mind, his handsome face and charming smile. For one second she savored the mental picture before thrusting it away. She would need a godmother with a magic wand if the Masters scion was to become a reality instead of a dream.

"Like Prince Charming for Cinderella," she quipped in an effort to combat the ache Maggie's words evoked. Long training in the sterile existence of her childhood made her take refuge in flippancy to hide any deep emotion.

"It could happen," Maggie affirmed seriously.

Jennifer's denial was automatic and emphatic. "Not to me. I'm a working girl. I'll meet someone someday. Don't worry." She glanced pointedly at her utilitarian watch. "We'd better get to work."

Maggie's disappointment was obvious. She knew from experience it was useless to try to force Jenny to change her mind about anything. "All right," she agreed finally. "Will you at least think about what I've said?"

Nodding, Jenny smiled gently. She was touched by Maggie's concern. The older woman was the closest thing she had to a mother. Seeking to soften Maggie's disappointment, she offered her a distraction she knew wouldn't fail. "I tell you what. Why don't we go shopping together after we close?"

Maggie's face lit up with enthusiasm. She eyed Jenny's tall, slender figure hopefully. "For you? A dress?" If there was one favorite pastime in Maggie's life, it was buying clothes. Whether for herself or someone else didn't matter one bit.

"Maybe even two. *And* if you talk to me nice, I just might try on something in lavender," Jenny offered with a laugh as she picked up the larger of the two packing boxes and headed for the back room.

The morning passed quickly, with hardly a break for either of them. It slacked off at lunch, allowing both of them to take an extended break together.

"I've been thinking," Maggie began determinedly.

"Oh, no," Jenny groaned, rolling her eyes heavenward in mock horror. She propped her denim-clad legs up on her workstool and settled back in her chair.

Ignoring Jenny's moans, Maggie leaned forward across the table, a gleam of fervor in her bright eyes. "You have the most fantastic coloring for dressing. Your light-brown hair with those strawberry highlights and those gray eyes are so unusual, they just cry out for attention.

"Whoever heard of a woman my age being chic with freckles?" Jenny pointed out. "I mean, the Doris Day image might have been all right in your day, but it isn't in mine."

"Don't kid yourself, honey. Sex is sex no matter what the generation. Do you young people think you're the only ones who ever heard of a relationship? My group invented the word, and what's more, we managed to make ours survive for years instead of days," she finished tartly.

Jenny struggled valiantly against the laughter bubbling inside her, but it wouldn't be squelched. She started to giggle, and once she began, she couldn't stop. Maggie was so serious and earnest, yet her words were out of character for what Jenny knew her to be: a dyed-in-the-wool romantic.

"You think it's funny. But it's not, and you know it. Look at you. You want marriage before bed. Because you think the only thing the 'modern male,'" Maggie snorted her disgust at the current vernacular, "is interested in is your body, you have virtually stopped dating."

"There's more to it than that," Jenny objected, suddenly as serious as Maggie.

"Agreed," Maggie replied with a quick nod of her gray head. "But don't you see, you won't find what you're looking for within the four walls of your apartment. You've got to get out, circulate, shine a little until you find someone who appeals to you. That's where the clothes come in, and the makeup."

"Makeup!" Jenny echoed in surprise. "Who said anything about cosmetics? I didn't!" She paused, eyeing Maggie's zealous face grimly. "I only remember mentioning the possible purchase of two dresses."

"I've changed my mind," Maggie shot back swiftly.

"*Your* mind?" Jenny's legs slid to the floor with a heavy thud as she sat up quickly. "What do you mean by that?" she demanded. "Maggie?" she prompted when the older woman didn't answer immediately.

"I mean it's about time I took your education in hand. Its something I've been wanting to do for a long time. You could be a stunning woman with just a little effort."

"Stunning?" She was beginning to sound like a parrot.

"Stunning," Maggie confirmed briskly. "Not beautiful, mind, but more interesting."

Jenny opened her mouth to refuse Maggie's well-meaning help, then shut it again as the sense of her words fully penetrated. Attractive? Her? Suddenly she wasn't so sure she wanted to forego this shopping trip, if for no other reason than to see her fairy godmother, Maggie, cope with board-straight brown hair and freckles.

Realistically, she knew there was no way she could become the woman Maggie described. Hadn't she lived with her faded coloring since she first saw her reflection in a mirror? All the clothes in the world weren't going to change this peasant into Cinderella.

3

I am *never* going shopping with you again as long as I live!" Jenny vowed fervently later that afternoon. Sinking wearily into a chair, she kicked off her shoes and surveyed Maggie with a jaundiced eye. "I'm exhausted—and you look like you haven't done a lick of work."

Maggie waved her hand at the mountain of packages scattered around Jenny's living room. "I haven't, child. You had to try on all that, *and* you're going to be the one putting it all away."

"Don't remind me. My ears are still ringing with line, fashion, flair and color. I never knew there was so much to choosing a simple dress. Or cosmetics." Jennifer gazed at Maggie curiously. "How do you know all those people we met this afternoon?"

Maggie grinned, obviously delighted with herself. "From when Bert and I owned that dress shop before we retired."

Jenny groaned aloud. "I should have guessed something like that." She caught Maggie's puzzled look. "You've probably been planning this since the day you started to work at the shop."

"Well, now I won't have anything to complain

about—at least in the clothes department," Maggie chuckled, rising to her feet. "I've got to be gettin' on home. Esmerelda will be wantin' her dinner."

Jenny followed her to the entrance foyer. "Thanks for your help Maggie." She touched the soft, feathered ends of her new hairstyle. "Especially for this. I never realized how much a simple thing like a body perm could do. I've always wanted curls," she admitted on a soft note.

"I told you you wouldn't recognize yourself. I bet you didn't even know how gorgeous your eyes are."

Jenny shook her head. "No, I didn't."

"Now maybe you'll get busy and get your prince, so I can dance at your wedding," she murmured teasingly.

As she shut the door behind Maggie, Jenny shook her head at her friend's persistent romantic fantasy. Maggie had Prince Charming on the brain. While she was deeply grateful for the knowledge and expertise Maggie had shown her, not to mention the patient instruction she had given, she couldn't imagine the future Maggie envisioned. It would have to be a very special man to overlook her lack of background. What man wanted to marry a woman with no name, no family, no knowledge of her own heritage. Her parents could have been anything . . . and probably were. Decent people didn't usually abandon their newborns by the river.

Jenny picked up a stack of boxes and carried them to her bedroom. Laying them on the bed, she began carefully putting away her new purchases. As she worked, she couldn't help thinking about the man she had met this morning.

He was so different from what she had expected. After having worked for his mother, Edna Masters, the past three years on the annual Dogwood Festival Ball, she thought she had a fairly good image of the

Masters clan. Daniel was surprisingly human in contrast to his more reserved mother. He was beyond her reach of course, she assured herself. But still . . . There was something about him that struck an answering cord within her.

"I'm getting as bad as Maggie," Jenny chided herself aloud when she realized the direction of her thoughts. Some of that stardust Maggie teased her about must have momentarily clouded her rational thinking. Daniel Masters was so far above her both in background and wealth as to make anything between them ridiculous. Besides, she wasn't a blonde.

Somehow the memory of the well-endowed Lilly Tyler provoked a giggle and restored her normal sense of proportion. Banishing Daniel Masters to the rarefied plane of the Masters' dynasty, Jennifer prepared and ate a light supper before dropping into bed.

The next morning Jenny rose a full half hour earlier than usual. After Maggie's instruction the day before, she intended to allow plenty of time to rework the magic she had been taught. Surprisingly, it was much simpler than she thought. Even her workday garb of jeans and a colorful cotton top became attractively stylish with the effect of her new haircut and the light makeup she used. She was well pleased with her efforts. So was Maggie when she entered the shop a short time later.

"I see you didn't have any trouble," she remarked, observing Jenny's handiwork with a critical eye.

Jenny grinned, her soft gray eyes glinting with devilry. "Not if you don't count the three tries at getting the kohl outlined around my eyes. I used up half the pencil."

Maggie chuckled as she headed for the front of the shop. "You'll get better with practice, don't worry."

"I certainly hope so," Jenny shot back swiftly.

"The price we women pay for beauty," Maggie mocked gently. "Now enough chatter. We've got work to do. And besides, for all you know, your prince may be coming through that door today."

Jenny giggled. "Oh, sure."

The morning brought an odd assortment of customers. Each time a presentable specimen of the male gender entered the front door, Maggie contrived to have an errand in the back, which left Jenny to serve the new arrival. By the time the afternoon rolled around, Jenny was hard put to keep a straight face at her friend's blatant matchmaking.

"You didn't like that one, either?" the older woman asked in disbelief after a particularly handsome football type departed.

"No," Jenny laughed as she clipped the man's order for a dozen red roses for his fiancée to her workboard. "I'm glad my customers don't know to what lengths you're prepared to go to snag me a mate."

"I just want to see—" The shrill ring of the telephone beside the register interrupted Maggie's comment. She picked it up and after a short conversation gestured for Jenny to speak to the caller.

"Mrs. Simpson," Maggie whispered as she passed her the receiver.

Recognizing the name of the secretary of the Dogwood Festival Ball's decorating committee, Jenny reached for a pad and pencil.

"Miss Brown, I'm so glad I caught you in. There's been a terrible mix-up. Our committee is meeting in an hour to discuss the details for the upcoming gala, and I just realized you hadn't been notified," the light, breezy voice in Jenny's ear hurried to explain. "Would it be at all possible for you to come over?"

"No problem, Mrs. Simpson," Jenny assured her

easily. Knowing how close the ball was, she had been expecting something like this for the past few days. Fortunately, she had made up a few of her ideas for floral decorations in silk flowers earlier in the week. It was a simple matter to transfer her samples to the van.

"I wonder what she would've done if you'd refused?" Maggie asked minutes later while helping Jenny collect her arrangements and sketch pad for ideas.

Jenny shrugged. "Gotten someone else. Half the stores in town would jump at the chance of working on the ball. Without Bessie's recommendation when I took over three years ago, I probably wouldn't have it anyway."

"In the beginning, but not now. I remember the enthusiastic response to your first efforts." Maggie eyed her denims skeptically when they slid the van doors shut on the last box. "Why don't you change into the gray slacks you bought yesterday? They would go great with that blouse."

Jennifer had forgotten about her new self. She glanced down at her clothes, suddenly dissatisfied with the collegiate look of her outfit. She definitely wanted to project a more businesslike image, and what better place to start than with one of the most prestigious social events of Knoxville. "Thanks for reminding me, Mag. I'll only be a minute," she called as she raced for the back stairs. Jeans or not, one did not keep the illustrious Mrs. Masters waiting.

Despite the delay, Jennifer arrived at the country club right on time and looking smart, even if she did say so herself. She nodded jauntily at the attractive stranger reflected in the van's rearview mirror. She darted her tongue over mauve-tinted lips before smiling at the image. Life was good—with or without Prince Charming, she decided.

Collecting her sample boxes and pad in her arms, she walked up the path to the awning-shaded entrance with its distinctive rose carpet. Her footsteps were muffled in the deep forest-green sculptured carpet as she crossed the anti-bellum-styled lobby area to the conference room on the left. She paused for a second at the closed door, admiring the attractive lobby, then knocked gently. Her summons was answered almost at once by the woman she had spoken to earlier.

"Miss Brown, you timed your arrival perfectly," Mrs. Simpson greeted her. "I believe you know everyone here."

Jennifer smiled politely while glancing over the well-dressed women seated around the circular table. With the exception of a very attractive doll-like blonde seated to the right of center, she had met everyone there. Her gaze lingered for a split second on Edna Masters in her place at the center of the group before she obeyed the secretary's silent gesture to be seated in the remaining empty chair. Placing her samples carefully in front of her, Jenny drew her notepad from her oversized leather bag.

"Ladies, you all know why we're here," Edna Masters began as soon as she saw Jenny was settled. "Now if I may recap, these are the arrangements we have made so far. We have chosen the night of April 14 for our little gala. . . ."

Giving half her attention to the clear, bell-like tones of the president, Jennifer took the opportunity of studying Daniel Masters' parent. In the three years she had worked with the elder Masters, she had never felt the least desire to know anything about her personally. Yet, now she found herself studying the older woman, looking for some resemblance to the handsome, golden-haired man she had met early one morning. There was none. No trace of the humanity she had glimpsed in the son marred the smooth perfection of the matte complexion. The even cadence of her speech showed no emotion while she calmly outlined the committee's plans for the upcoming ball. *Her* plans, no doubt, Jenny hazarded shrewdly when the elegantly coiffed heads of the members nodded agreement with each of her proposals.

When called upon, Jenny described her own thoughts on the decorations, and then listened in surprise as her ideas were adopted with unanimous approval.

"Shall we adjourn to the ballroom, ladies?" Although the words carried the intonation of a question, it was obeyed as a supreme command.

Jennifer rose obediently and followed the group to the vast room where the annual function was held. As many times as she had been inside the elegant chamber—it was too much of a place stolen from a forgotten era to be called anything so mundane as a room—she was still impressed by the sheer size. From the ornate gold and crystal chandelier-draped ceiling to the never-ending expanse of polished wood floor, it whispered of bygone days of chivalry, of lovely southern belles and handsome, dashing escorts.

Jenny strolled slowly around, noting the newly painted pale cream walls with satisfaction. The daffodils she planned for a border around the orchestra dais would be perfect. She counted the tables inside and then stepped outside on the terrace and found a few had been added since the year before. She made note of the changes.

"Cynthia dear, would you come here?"

At the sound of Edna Masters' voice, Jennifer glanced up from her sketch pad where she had been drawing in the new seating arrangements. She saw the petite blonde detach herself from a trio of older women and glide across the floor in response to the soft-spoken summons.

"Yes, Edna?"

Jenny's brow climbed in silent amazement at the familiar tone of the drawling question. She wondered who the woman was. Everyone in Knoxville knew Daniel and his mother were the last of the line, so she couldn't be a relative, at least not a close one.

From what Jennifer had observed, hardly anyone addressed Mrs. Masters in anything but the most formal terms. Yet this woman dared, and what's more, drew a smile from the perfectly poised matriarch.

"Hello again."

Startled, Jenny spun around, nearly dropping her pad, and found herself confronting an amused pair of blue eyes.

"Mr. Masters," she stammered. "I didn't hear you come up." She glanced around the empty terrace in bewilderment. "How . . ."

". . . did I get here?" he finished for her. He gestured toward the far end of the railed balcony and the half-hidden door, which Jenny knew led to the lobby. "Now, since I answered your question, suppose you tell me what you're doing here, Jenny Brown."

Jenny met the probing curiosity of Daniel's vivid blue eyes with difficulty. Their last encounter was one she preferred to forget.

Daniel stood casually at her side, either unknowing or uncaring that they could be seen by the women of the committee. "Well, I'm waiting."

Jenny wondered what unlucky star governed her fate in this man's presence. The last thing she wanted to do was admit her reason for being at the club. Her lashes flickered briefly, shielding her thoughts from the man watching her so intently. For one insane moment she debated lying. She opened her eyes, their soft gray depths gone silver with the composure she gathered about her. If he intended to denounce her to his mother and her cronies for the part she played in Lilly's joke, then so be it.

"I'm here to discuss the floral arrangements for the ball," she explained in a cool, precise voice she hardly recognized as her own.

One tawny brow rose expressively, mirroring the skeptical look in his eyes. He studied her a moment before his gaze dropped to the sketch pad she still held.

Jennifer saw him register the sketches of her decorating ideas. With his comprehension, his face hardened, the handsome features growing taut with restrained emotion. She had seen him angry, puzzled and amused. Now she caught a glimpse of the financial genius who had parlayed a small family fortune into a far-reaching empire.

"So, you aren't as innocent as you would have me believe. I should have known Lilly didn't think up that little masterpiece on her own."

Amazement vied with disbelief as Jenny stared at her accuser in shock. The icy inflection in his voice sent shivers of apprehension through her. This was much worse than anything she could possibly imagine.

Glaring into the face hovering above her, she opened her lips to refute his unjust charge, but she wasn't given a chance to utter a syllable in her own defense.

"Daniel, dahling, you're late." A light, childishly sweet voice shattered the tense silence between Daniel and Jennifer.

As one, they swung to confront the tiny blonde coming toward them. "A reprieve," Daniel murmured in a low-toned promise of later retribution that only Jenny could hear.

"Cynthia," he greeted the newcomer warmly, the anger erased from his voice and his expression. He took the delicate hand she extended, smiling indulgently as his lips brushed the scented cheek she offered him.

Jenny admired his self-control even while she disliked the ease with which he used it.

"I didn't know you had met Miss Brown," the younger girl commented vaguely.

Daniel's eyes flickered dismissively over Jennifer's still form before returning to Cynthia's openly admiring face. "Once," he acknowledged with a shrug.

Jennifer breathed a soft sigh of relief at the brief reply. Some of the tension in her body ebbed.

Seeing the arrival of the blonde as a chance to escape, Jenny seized the opportunity. If Daniel meant to betray her part in Lilly's gesture—a role she freely admitted she regretted—she wanted to be gone when he did it. She had been foolish to participate in such a prank to begin with. From a business point of view, if from no other, it was a stupid thing to do.

"If you will excuse me," she murmured politely, "I need to have a word with Mrs. Masters about the flowers."

"We wouldn't want to keep you from your work," Cynthia agreed guilelessly. She slid a slender hand through the crook in Daniel's arm and leaned against him. "Would we?"

"If you say so, honey." Daniel flicked a look at the expensively thin watch on his left wrist before glancing up, neatly snagging Jenny's eyes. "We should be going ourselves."

For a moment, Jenny was powerless to combat the compelling force of his hard, sapphire stare. He had the power to hurt her livelihood with only one word, and they both knew it. Unknowingly, Jenny's eyes reflected her anxiety and her desire to flee. A muscle twitched along the tanned cheek as Daniel released his visual hold, freeing her frozen limbs.

It took every ounce of Jennifer's acquired poise to walk, not run, to Mrs. Masters' side and coherently discuss floral centerpieces she might never be called upon to make. With each passing second the enormity of what she had done loomed larger, growing totally out of proportion in her worried mind.

She scarcely noticed her drive back to the shop. One thought was emblazoned on her brain: Daniel Masters and the circle he led made up over three-fourths of her business. Without him and his group there would be no Garden of Eden. No home, no life. The end of everything she had worked so hard to achieve.

After all, what customer wanted to deal with a shop that parodied its own services for someone's personal vendetta. The possibility of such a practice was enough to make her rich clientele drop their silver spoons. And all it needed was one word from Daniel Masters, Jennifer acknowledged in despair. One word! She could almost hear the polite little phone call from Mrs. Simpson that would herald the beginning of the end.

But there was none. Not the following day, or the day after, or the one after that. The business remained remarkably tranquil. Not so were Jenny's thoughts. With each passing hour a conviction grew within her that she owed Daniel an apology and an explanation. Not just because she feared what he might do, but also because her conscience demanded it.

The problem was how to go about seeing him. His office was the logical place, but she would need an

appointment, which he very well might not grant.
And there they would be subject to interruptions.

The problem nagged at her mind as Jenny guided
the van through the early Friday evening traffic. She
ran a hand wearily over her tousled hair and down
the back of her neck. It had been a long day, with
Billy out sick again. The last delivery across town had
been a late one.

As she stopped at a red light, some impulse made
her flip her right blinker on and turn the corner. Two
blocks, and the blunt nose of the truck eased into the
empty parking lot of the Masters building. Still
guided by an unseen hand, she swung the van
around the back of the complex where the execu-
tives parked their cars. The sight of the low-slung
silver Porsche in the slot nearest the rear door didn't
surprise her. Somehow she had known he would be
here.

After parking her flower-decked truck a few spaces
away, Jenny slid from the seat. Just as she was about
to lock her door, her eyes fell on the small cluster of
roses, carnations and mums she habitually carried as
extras in case an arrangement was damaged en-
route.

Of its own volition, her hand reached for the single
rose in the center of the bouquet. Snow white as the
dove of peace, it was the perfect offering: a living
apology for her former visit.

4

This time there was no Penny to greet her as Jenny entered Daniel's outer office. She was alone, although she almost hadn't been. It had taken a lot of talking to convince the night watchman she wasn't a trespasser. Pausing at Penny's desk, Jenny took a deep, calming breath. She never felt more like running away in her life. Her hand tightened on the slender stem of the flower she held, causing her to wince in pain as a thorn pricked her thumb. Transferring the rose to her other hand, she raised her finger to her mouth.

At that moment, the door to Daniel's private sanctum swung open. Jennifer found herself staring at the man she had come to see. Every word she planned to say flew right out of her mind.

"Oh, Lord," she breathed as she slowly removed her finger.

"Is that a case of mistaken identity, or a prayer?" Daniel drawled. He leaned his shoulder against the door jam and surveyed her lazily.

Ignoring his jibe, Jenny tried to read his expression, but failed. His lashes drooped over his eyes, screening his thoughts from her view. She swallowed resolutely and took a step forward.

"I came to talk to you. To try to explain . . ." she began.

"Yes?" he questioned unhelpfully.

Jenny hesitated, not sure how to continue. She hated the idea of blurting out the whole story right here in the middle of Penny's office. The outer door wasn't even closed.

"You might as well come into my office," he suggested expressionlessly, seeing her hesitation.

Expecting him to move aside for her to enter, Jenny was disconcerted to find he only turned slightly to allow her to pass. Her shoulder brushed his chest as she went by, making her suddenly conscious of how much taller he was than she had realized. His lean build was deceptive. She felt his presence behind her like a hovering shadow while she crossed the deep blue pile carpet. She took a seat in one of the two leather chairs in front of the sleek mahogany desk. The flower she had so impulsively brought lay in her lap. She waited until he sat down before she spoke.

Raising serious smoky eyes, Jennifer faced him. "I've come to apologize and, hopefully, if you'll let me, try to explain my actions," she stated simply. She paused, hands clenched around the stem of the rose, for his decision. She thought she caught a flicker of surprise in the probing blue eyes, but it was gone so quickly she couldn't be certain.

"I'm listening."

He hadn't changed his watchful attitude by a fraction of an inch, yet Jenny felt his curiosity.

"I'll need to start a little before I met Lilly. It may take some time," she warned.

His lips twisted in a sardonic grin. "We have all

night." He leaned back in his chair in a relaxed attitude.

Taking a deep breath, Jenny squared her shoulders as though she were facing a judge—which in a way she was, she admitted wryly.

"As you probably know by now, I own the Garden of Eden Florist Shop. Ever since I took over three years ago, I've been doing the annual Dogwood Festival Ball, but I've also done many of the floral arrangements ordered from this office . . . from you." Her eyes dropped for a moment to her hands. Seeing the tense whiteness of her fingers, she forced them open. "I'm not proud of myself, believe me. But when I delivered those yellow roses to Miss Tyler, suddenly the gesture of that bouquet of flowers you always send to your girlfriends hit me."

She heard the hiss of his indrawn breath, and she raised her head. "I know I shouldn't have made a judgment—"

"You're damned right you shouldn't," he bit out harshly.

She flinched at the cutting lash of his tongue and fell silent. She wished her conscience had been a lot less active. This hard-eyed man bore little resemblance to the man she had first met.

"You've gotten this far. Go on," he commanded tersely.

"Lilly . . . Miss Tyler was angry when I left. She was waiting for me when I opened the shop the next morning. When she told me why she had come, I'll admit I thought it was a funny way of making a point."

"Women!" A world of masculine disgust was contained in the one word epitaph.

Meeting his eyes steadily, Jenny braved the twin blue flames of gathering anger. She had vowed she would tell the whole truth if she got the chance. She intended to fulfill that promise.

A slight flush rose in Jenny's cheeks at his remark, but she forced herself to finish. "I told Lilly I wouldn't do what she originally planned, but I would arrange the wild flowers and take them to your office. I didn't charge her."

"Is that supposed to mean something?"

"I thought it did at the time. Now I know I was fooling myself," she admitted in a low voice. "I shouldn't have gotten involved."

"Just because you didn't take any money for what you did doesn't mean you're in the clear," he commented caustically.

Jenny's head came up with a snap at his accurate reading of her motives. He smiled mockingly at her expression. "You don't need to look so startled. It wasn't hard to figure out."

The sarcastic taunt scraped along Jenny's already lacerated conscience. A slow anger began to build, overshadowing her desire to make amends. To apologize and to explain was one thing; to debase herself before this arrogant male was another. Nothing, not even her business, was worth losing her self-respect. Why should she care whether she had hurt him? What was he to her, anyway? Certainly neither lover nor friend. The soft gray eyes of remorse glazed silver as she stared across the width of his desk.

When Daniel saw the change in her, his own eyes narrowed. "Just what was Lilly's first plan?" he asked in a tone that brooked no argument.

"She was going to have her farewell to you delivered at your eleven o'clock board meeting," Jenny snapped, goaded. She was beginning to wish she had delivered the blasted chamber pot right in front of his board meeting. It would do him good to know a little of the discomfort she was now feeling.

Daniel's face went blank with amazement at the picture Jenny's brief words had drawn. "I'll be damned!" The purely masculine comment echoed in the silence of the room.

Searching blue eyes probed the glittering silver depths, seeing the temper reflected there. His lips twitched suspiciously.

Jenny's expression mirrored some of Daniel's amazement when she saw him smile. She stared at him, unable to believe the abrupt change in him.

"It seems I owe you an apology, Jenny Brown," Daniel drawled.

"Really?" she asked hopefully, feeling a slight easing of her guilt over her participation.

"Yes, really. One of the partners in a company I am looking over is a real dyed-in-the-wool stickler on morality. The last thing he'd understand would be Lilly's temperamental dramatics. Besides, he hasn't got a sense of humor," he finished thoughtfully.

Jenny couldn't stifle the giggle bubbling within her at his last comment. She recalled a decided lack of that same virtue in Daniel.

"Maybe it's a masculine failing," she suggested, her eyes gleaming with sudden teasing. In his suddenly more approachable mood, Daniel aroused no fears in her.

For a long moment, Daniel gazed at her, neither reacting to her amusement or offering any comment.

Jenny felt the sweep of his assessing regard and wondered what had put the almost speculative look in the blue depths of his eyes. Her grin faded as she shifted restlessly.

"Yes, well . . ." he murmured finally, his lips curving into a wry smile. "Let's just say shock temporarily paralyzed my funnybone."

Relieved, Jenny banished the vague stirrings of

unease. She had imagined his odd look, she assured herself. "Am I forgiven?" she asked in a rush. For days she had agonized over this meeting. Now it was nearly finished, and she needed Daniel's verbal absolution. Then she and her persistent conscience would be back to normal.

Daniel appeared to consider. "I might, for a forfeit."

Bemused, Jenny shook her head at the teasing quality of his slow, deep voice. She glanced down at her hands to give herself time to think. What was he playing at? Suddenly she focused on the forgotten rose she held.

She lifted it carefully and placed it on the desk between them.

"Will this do?" she asked quietly.

At her gesture, all the amusement in Daniel's face died. His gaze locked on her for a second before dropping to the perfect white flower, her peace offering.

Without surprise she watched Daniel lift the partially unfurled bloom and gently touch one velvety petal. Her breath caught in her throat at the caressing stroke of his finger on the rose. A flicker of a previously unexperienced desire shot through her. Her tongue flickered out to moisten her tingling lips. The scent of the rose swirled around her, tantalizing her senses. She raised her eyes and found herself drowning in the blue pools of warmth so near.

"Will you have dinner with me tonight?" Daniel's husky question floated across the space dividing them.

"Yes," Jenny agreed softly. An instinct she hardly recognized prompted her answer.

He nodded and got to his feet still holding the rose. "Let's go, then."

At his words, reality came crashing back. Jenny stood up, making an expressive gesture at her casual work clothes. "I'm not really—"

"—dressed," he finished, as he took her arm in a firm grip. "Neither am I. Where we're going, it won't matter."

Casting him a sidelong glance, Jenny realized in surprise he was telling the truth. In her haste to explain herself, she had been blind to everything around her. She saw Daniel, too, was wearing denims—designer, of course, but well washed. The light blue fabric stretched across lean hips and down his long legs without a crease. A soft cream turtle-neck pullover, a perfect complement to the tawny gold hair, hugged the deceptively wide shoulders. He looked sleek, sophisticated and totally in command. Jenny's sleeping senses stirred to life. Here was her fantasy, the dream of a lonely girl's heart. The woman in her warned her to be wary.

As she matched his long strides through the empty corridors, she questioned her sanity at accepting Daniel's invitation. It had been an extremely busy day even with the late delivery. She was tired. While Daniel said good-bye to the night watchman as he locked them out of the darkened building, she debated how to tell him she wasn't going with him. When they reached his Porsche, she turned to face him.

"I've changed my—" Jenny got out just before Daniel took advantage of her parted lips with a surprising kiss. One of her hands was crushed against his chest, and when she tried to push him away with the other, he caught it easily in his free hand. Tethered by the strength of his arm about her waist, Jenny was unable to do more than struggle helpless-ly as his warm mouth plundered hers. His kiss stole her breath, as well as her refusal, and all she could think of in that instant was the persuasive, possessive power of his lips.

It was over almost at once, leaving Jenny gasping while she rested her forehead against his shoulder. The warmth of his body penetrated her clothes while he held her against him. Her trapped hand telegraphed the deep, accelerated throb of his heart, betraying his arousal.

"I won't let you back out, Jenny," he murmured softly against her ear. "We have a date, don't we?"

Jenny nodded mutely, unable to voice her agreement. Being pressed against Daniel the way she was played havoc with her senses. Every breath he drew, every movement he made was instantly transmitted to her own traitorous body and she, heaven help her, was aware of it.

Retaining a grip of her hand, Daniel released her slowly almost as if he were afraid she would try to escape. He handed her the rose, then he opened the car door and gently pushed her inside.

Bewildered and confused by her almost immediate physical reaction to his caress, Jenny remained silent until he slid into the driver's seat and started the engine.

"Why?" she asked in a husky voice that betrayed the effect his kiss had on her.

Daniel shrugged lightly, his eyes touching her briefly before he turned his attention to his driving. "I don't really know," he murmured at last. A wry grin lifted his lips. "An impulse?"

Impulse! Jenny echoed silently. He kissed her for that? She would have sworn Daniel Masters was the last person to give in to spur-of-the-moment actions. Yet the total lack of a smooth answer carried its own ring of truth. A man with his experience was rarely, if ever, at a loss for words. Could he be prey to the same chaotic feelings as she?

Unable to make sense of her own reactions, Jenny shifted slightly in her seat so she could study Daniel as he drove. The flickering light of the passing street lamps illuminated his clearcut features, sculpting the distinctive expressionless planes with silver. Defeated by the smooth contours of the blank mask, Jenny sank back in the plush cushioning of expensive leather, hoping the silence in the interior of the Porsche would calm her. She wanted to run a mile away from him, but she couldn't summon the strength of will to do it. There were two people inside her at war with each other, the daydreaming Jennifer and the more practical Jenny.

Daniel was apparently as lost in thought as she, she realized when she took another sidelong peek at him through her lashes. She wondered if his feelings were as confused as hers.

By the time Daniel guided the car into the large dirt parking lot of Tim's Bar-B-Que, Jenny felt more able to cope with the evening ahead. The brief silent drive had given her a chance to recover some of her natural composure.

"I've never been here before," she remarked conversationally when she slid from the car.

"A friend of mine owns it."

Jenny breathed a mental sigh of relief at the casual response. It appeared he was as ready as she was to forget about the incident outside his building.

He took her arm, guiding her toward the squat rustic building in front of them. The pungent odor of roasting meat mixed with hickory filled the air, making Jenny realize how hungry she was.

"They must do a thriving business," she commented as she and Daniel entered. She glanced around appreciatively. The long dining room was reminiscent of a country kitchen with pine trestle tables, high-backed benches and old-fashioned blue onion crockery. The atmosphere was cozily home-like and surprisingly intimate.

"Best ribs in Knoxville," Daniel agreed. He smiled a greeting at the hostess. "Is Tim around?"

"In the kitchen," she replied, leading the way to a table. She handed them the menus after they took their seats. "I'll tell him you're here."

Daniel nodded, thanking her with a smile. "Do you prefer beef or pork?"

"Both," Jenny supplied with a teasing grin. "I'm starving. It must be that lunch I missed."

The waitress materialized at their table. "We'll have the assorted special," he ordered, taking her at her word. He turned to Jenny, "Beer all right with you? Coffee after?"

"Lovely."

"Well, as I live and breathe, Danny boy!" The hearty greeting rang across the dining area, drawing several customers' eyes as well as Daniel and Jenny's attention. A large bear of a man lumbered toward them.

Daniel rose, confronting the white-aproned figure who extended a pawlike hand. Jenny was surprised at the exuberant welcome afforded a man of Daniel's standing. And even more so when it was recipro-cated.

"This is Jenny Brown, Tim," Daniel supplied when the greetings finally subsided. "I'm introducing her to your specialty for the first time, so mind your pots, my friend."

A deep chuckle rumbled through the massive chest of the proprietor. "Okay, little man, behold me quakin' in me boots. I'll depart and see to the feedin' of your maid." With an unbelievably graceful bow, Tim strolled toward the swinging doors of the open pit kitchen.

Jenny, her mouth slightly agape, stared after him. She hadn't had a chance to do more than smile an acknowledgment of her introduction during the extraordinary meeting.

Seeing her expression, Daniel laughed. "You can close your mouth. The food won't be here for a while."

"Little man?" she questioned faintly, scarcely hearing his order. "He's at least four inches shorter than you."

"And about seventy-five pounds heavier." Daniel lifted his beer and took a sip. "He was my center when we played football for Bear Bryant and the Crimson Tide."

"You played for the University of Alabama?"

He nodded. "Where did you go to school?"

"Here in town," Jenny shrugged evasively, not wanting to admit her lack of education. Living in a college town where nearly everyone had a degree had made her self-conscious about having only a high school diploma. She had wanted so desperately to get a B.S. in horticulture, but even with the night classes at the college she had managed to sandwich into her busy schedule and tight pocketbook, she still had a way to go.

"So we were rivals," he concluded. "What was your major?"

Suddenly Jenny found the contents of her beer glass eye-riveting and she avoided Daniel's gaze. She hated the feeling of inadequacy that assailed her. "I didn't go to college," she admitted in a low voice.

"Why not?" he asked gently, sensing her distress.

Annoyance at his probing darkened her eyes to

slate as she lifted her head. It wasn't his fault he had hit a sensitive nerve, yet she couldn't suppress the desire to snap.

"Orphans aren't given an education allowance for higher learning no matter how good their grades are. Even student loans require some guarantee of later payment, and I couldn't give that."

Ignoring her ill-temper, Daniel digested her blunt statement in silence for a moment. "I take it you never knew your parents?" he questioned, changing the subject slightly.

Backed into a corner by Daniel's persistent digging into her past, Jenny took refuge in flippancy to hide her feelings. "In the manner of Moses, someone placed her newborn in a wicker laundry basket and left it in the park by the river one night. It was a nice summer evening, so the next morning my noisy squalls attracted the attention of one of the city employees who policed the grounds. He found the basket and turned it in. There was no name or note attached to what little I was wearing so the authorities were called in. Naturally, the police tried to locate my donor, but . . ." Jenny trailed to a stop and shrugged expressively. She waited, expecting some comment. Daniel arched a questioning brow, his silence a command for her to finish the story.

Wishing now she hadn't started the conversation, Jenny plunged ahead. "I spent a couple of years in the state home before I started the foster parents round. I wasn't an attractive child," she explained as though making a profound observation. The hurt of those early years of rejection and moving from one family to another colored her voice, betraying the young Jenny's bewilderment at the harsh realities of life. "I was a bit of a hell-raiser, too."

"I'm not surprised," Daniel commented wryly. "What happened after that?"

Jenny gave a twisted grin. "Nothing much. They just quit trying to palm me off on every family that walked through the door. I was getting too old, anyway. By then I was thirteen. At least, I think I was. One of the advantages of being a foundling is being able to pick your own birthday."

Daniel's eyes gleamed with laughter at the satisfaction in Jenny's voice. "I wonder why I have a feeling the date you chose had some significance?" He studied her face for a moment, enjoying the silver flashes of humor from her remarkable eyes. "July fourth," he pronounced triumphantly.

Jenny could only stare at him in silence. How could he understand the child's desperate lie of independence from her parents, whoever they were, instead of the abandonment it really was?

"Your order, ma'am."

Jenny started visibly at the waitress's voice at her side. The heaping plate of homemade french fries, garlic bread and thick, juicy ribs was a welcome diversion. Daniel's uncanny ability to read her mind was unnerving. How did he see so much in so little time? It was hard to believe that a man with his affluent background could be so easy to be with, so in tune to her thoughts.

For years Daniel had been the man of her dreams, the one by whom she had unconsciously measured all others. Yet here, now, the fantasy was real, and more than her wildest imaginings could ever have been.

"How did you guess?" she blurted out once they were alone again.

Daniel turned his golden head, fixing her with an amused stare. "That you chose Independence Day?"

She nodded.

"Intuition?"

She arched her brow in mute demand for further explanation.

"Because it's what I would have done myself, I suppose, if I'd been abandoned," he replied thoughtfully. He saw her flinch at his bluntness. His gaze was warmly understanding. "Your parents are the losers, Jenny, not you. They missed seeing a very special child grow to womanhood." He smiled gently at the pale blush that rose in her cheeks at his compliment. Taking pity on her obvious embarrassment, he bent his head and picked up his fork.

At a loss over how to deal with the man across from her, Jenny seized eagerly on the food in front of her as a topic of conversation. Anything was better than this scary, almost telepathic communication between them.

"This looks fabulous," she commented. "If it tastes as good as it smells, I may never eat barbecue anywhere else."

For a time neither spoke while they did full justice to Tim's excellent fare. When the waitress came to take away their empty plates and the small pile of bare bones left from their feast, she also brought the coffee Daniel had ordered earlier.

"What happened after you finished high school?" Daniel asked when they were alone again.

"Don't you ever give up?" Jenny countered, becoming irritated at his persistent probing.

He shook his head, his face mirroring some of the determination he exercised in his business life. "Not when it's important."

"And this is?" She picked up her coffee and met his gaze over the rim of the mug.

An odd flicker of uncertainty flitted across his expression for a second before he shrugged evasively. "What's wrong with my knowing?" he asked instead.

"I just don't like people prying into my life. Is that so hard to understand? How would you like it if I probed into your past?"

"What do you want to know? I'm single, past the age of consent and relatively well off."

At the last very underestimated quality, Jenny choked on her sip of coffee. "Well off?" she questioned incredulously.

"Wealthy, then, if it makes you feel any better." He reached across the table and took the cup from her hands. "Now it's your turn."

Jenny glared her exasperation. He wasn't going to let her escape his inquisition no matter how much she fought it. Better to give him the bare details and hope he would be satisfied, she decided. She thought longingly of her van, wishing it were outside instead of across town.

"I finished high school and went to work for old Mrs. Griffin. She offered me the managerial position and later let me buy her out. That's how I got the Garden of Eden," she replied briefly.

"I remember."

Jenny looked at him suspiciously. "What do you mean?"

Daniel grinned. "My mother nearly went into shock when you took over. She was so accustomed to working with Mrs. Griffin, at first she was sure she would need to find a new florist." He paused tantalizingly.

"And?" she prompted urgently.

"Now she's wondering how she ever did without your services."

Unconsciously, Jenny had been holding her breath. Hearing his words, she let it out in a soft sigh. "Thank heavens," she murmured in relief. Thinking of the Masters matriarch reminded Jenny of her indiscretion of the chamber pot. "Why didn't you tell your mother what I did?" she asked curiously.

Daniel grimaced distastefully, a brief flare of anger lighting his eyes. "Do I look like someone who runs for cover when he gets his feelings hurt?" he demanded.

She shook her head. "No, of course not."

His rigid body relaxed at her immediate denial. "I didn't tell her because it wasn't any of her business. It didn't affect your work on her charity functions so—"

"Yes, but it did reflect on my business integrity—" she began, but he interrupted her.

"I think you worry too much about that. So you made a mistake. Big deal. You've explained and apologized—very nicely, I might add. Now let it go."

Jenny opened her lips to comment further, but his admonitory finger against their parted fullness drove what she was going to say right out of her head.

"Not another word. Okay?" His vivid eyes commanded her agreement. When she gave it, he smiled approvingly.

"I like the new hairstyle," he observed as he took his hand away. "It suits you."

Confused by the complete change of subject, Jenny responded absently. "It was Maggie's idea." He quirked an eyebrow curiously. "My assistant in the shop," she explained.

At his urging, she went on to relate the highlights of Maggie's and her assault on the Knoxville merchants. Exposed to the full scope of the Masters' charm, she relaxed enough to laugh with Daniel at Maggie's antics. Jenny was amazed at how quickly the evening sped by. Conversing with Daniel was a surprising mixture of humor and intensity. In spite of their diverse backgrounds, they shared many interests and beliefs. It was almost closing time when Daniel finally paid the bill and escorted her to the car.

With a sigh, Jenny leaned back in the plush leather seat, allowing the comfortable bucket to cradle her pleasantly weary body. She closed her eyes briefly, deciding the evening had gone pretty well after the initially bad start.

There was a faint click, then the raspy velvet voice of Kenny Rogers filled the interior of the car. The low stereo music was soothing. Floating in a sea of dark warmth, Jenny began to hum softly in time to the melody.

"Do you know the words?" Daniel's question was clear enough to be heard without intruding on the tranquil mood.

Jenny's lashes lifted slightly as she turned her head to stare at his profile. "Yes," she admitted.

Daniel slanted her a quick look, his mouth curving into a smile at the relaxed expression on her face. "Sing it for me?" It was half command and part request.

"You might wish you hadn't asked that," she replied with a grin before obligingly picking up the beat. This was one of her favorite songs and one she had often vocalized with on her van's radio and at home. The slightly husky throb in her voice was a perfect complement to the singer. The force of her awareness of the man beside her lent the lyrical love song a depth and poignancy in keeping with the beautiful words.

"You're really good," Daniel stated as the music faded gently to a close. "Have you ever thought about turning pro?"

Smiling, Jenny shook her head. "Not me. I enjoy singing. I even play a fairly decent guitar, but I haven't the interest or the ambition to do more. It's a pleasant, satisfying hobby."

"No desire to be rich and famous?"

Jenny heard the seriousness underlying the teasing question.

"Nope." She chuckled at his skeptical expression. "I have no wish to set the world on fire. I want a nice life, nothing special. A home, a husband, a couple of kids and enough money to pay the bills without worrying where my next meal is coming from." She frowned thoughtfully at the passing streets. For a moment she forgot the man beside her and what he represented. "I know I don't want to be wealthy. I like the challenge of succeeding, of building a place for myself too much. I don't want the complacency that could come with being able to have anything and everything I wished." Faintly embarrassed with the revealing depth of her answer, Jenny lapsed into silence. What on earth had prompted her to open her mind and her heart once again to this man? Hadn't she learned through bitter experience to keep her own counsel? Never in her life had she told one human being so much about herself.

"Thank you."

Startled at the soft-spoken comment, Jennifer glanced at Daniel to find him turned slightly toward her. Lost in thought, she hadn't realized they had arrived at their destination. "For what?" she asked curiously.

Daniel lifted one hand to trace the clean line of her jaw from her ear to her chin. "For not making some stupid, social comment." Seeing the bewilderment in her gray eyes, he explained. "I've never met anyone like you. You're honest, direct, and you've got courage. You've started from very little and made a special place for yourself. I admire that. I admire *you*."

Jenny's cheeks flushed a delicate pink at the unusual compliment. If she was surprised at his eloquence, she was even more so by her reaction to it. She studied him intently, supremely conscious of the warmth of his hand against her face. What was this current of awareness running between them?

"I'm not usually so . . . so . . ." She trailed self-consciously to a stop. How could she explain her openness to him when she didn't understand it herself.

". . . forthcoming," Daniel supplied, seeing her hesitation.

She nodded mutely, scarcely aware of gripping her hands tightly together in her lap. The restricted confines of the car and the dimly lit parking lot combined to form an isolation made provocative by Daniel's nearness. It was all she could do to keep from leaning against the chest so enticingly close. She felt the comforting strength of his hand as it covered hers and eased the clenched fingers open. Jenny stared into Daniel's face, visually tracing the strong, clean lines of his bone structure, the golden-winged brows hovering above deep indigo pools. How was it she could know such an irresistible yearning for this man's touch? She had never felt like this in her life. It was frightening in its intensity. There was no future for her here. She sensed it with a well-developed survival instinct, yet she was unable to pull away.

"You're feeling it too, aren't you?" Daniel's voice was a rough whisper of a truth Jennifer desperately wanted to deny. He moved closer, his lips just inches away from hers. "How did it happen?" he murmured. Clearly he expected no answer, and he got none.

Surprised at his perception and yet in a way not, Jennifer was incapable of a reply. His gaze awoke a need in her to know his touch, to be in his arms again. She leaned toward him.

For a split second, Daniel resisted her invitation. Then, he sighed, and his arms encircled her pliant body as his mouth claimed hers.

Where before his caress had caught her unawares and she had fought it, now Jenny responded fully to the pressure of his lips.

Daniel took his time, gently teasing for entry into the dark cave holding the mysteries of her. His tongue probed and searched the hidden recesses, learning her secrets and granting her knowledge of him in return.

Jenny felt his need and trembled before the onslaught of burgeoning emotions. When his hand went to her swelling breast, she moaned in pleasure, arching against his questing fingers.

"No," Daniel tore his mouth away, his breath a ragged rasp filling the car. "No! Not here! Not now!" His arms, so recently binding bands of velvet, were rigid as he held Jennifer away from him.

Stunned, Jenny sank weakly back against her seat. Smoky gray eyes the color of the early morning mists across the river fastened on Daniel's tautly controlled features. What had she done, she questioned in despair. What on earth had prompted her to allow this? Allow? That was a laugh. Invite? Ask? She had done everything but say she wanted him. She closed her eyes on the bitter thought. Where were her fine principles now?

"Jenny, look at me," he commanded, his voice betraying his own aroused state. "I mean it; open your eyes."

Unwillingly, Jenny's lashes lifted to find him staring at her, understanding of her feelings written clearly on his face.

"There's nothing to be ashamed about," he began quietly, making no move to close the distance between them or to touch her in any way. "Nothing

73

happened, except for a moment we both forgot what we are and became just a man and a woman drawn to each other."

Could he really mean what he was saying? Was he holding her background against her? Hearing his voice, she realized he was speaking again.

"I'm thirty-six years old. I don't marry my women, Jenny. I don't need to." He paused on the deliberately harsh assessment, then his voice gentled slightly. "But you're not like all the others. You want all the trappings. You want all the things you missed as a child. The security, the love, and someone to belong to. That's good for you, but it's not my way. I can't give you that commitment. Don't waste your dreams on a man like me. God knows we would be good, in spite of your inexperience, but neither of us would be happy with what came later—the recriminations, the disillusionment. Maybe I could change your mind if I tried hard enough, but I'm not going to. I've passed the age where every woman I meet is a challenge. I know my track record doesn't bear me out, but it's true, nonetheless." He watched her, his brutally honest eyes steady on her expressive face. "Can you understand what I'm saying?"

She didn't question his assertion that he could make her reverse her opinion, especially considering her response the moment before. Reading the finality, the ruthless determination in his aristocratic features, Jenny knew he spoke the truth. In a way, she was relieved. To end it now before it began was best for both of them, not only for the reasons he mentioned. If by some miracle they did come to mean something to each other, she couldn't see Edna Masters or any of that group ever pretending to accept someone like her. She went cold at the idea.

"Yes, Daniel, I understand," she answered quietly,

using his name for the first time. "You have your way and I have mine."

For a moment longer he held her gaze, then nodded as if satisfied.

"You're a very special lady, Jenny Brown, whoever your people were. When you find your man, he's going to be very lucky to have your love."

Daniel's smile of approval dispelled some of the chill surrounding her.

He put out his right hand. "Friends?"

"Friends," Jenny echoed softly, placing her own capable hand in his and feeling the warmth of his grasp enfold her fingers. She smiled, suddenly calm and at peace, his words somehow healing an ache within her. She didn't analyze why; she simply accepted it.

Daniel slid out of his seat, came around to her side of the car and opened the door. Accepting his company silently, Jenny couldn't think of a single thing to say as he took her keys and unlocked the driver's side of the van. He handed the key chain to her and stepped back.

Jenny quickly slipped up onto the seat and shut the door.

"Good-bye, Jenny Brown," he drawled softly, his vivid eyes on a level with her own. For a second, there was a tiny flicker of fire in the indigo depths before the mask of the Masters scion slipped into place. She watched him walk slowly around his Porsche and stop by his door to lean one arm on the silver top.

"No more yellow roses for good-bye." His grin of self-mockery flashed white in the illumination of the parking lot light.

There was an unaccustomed sting of tears in Jenny's eyes as she returned his smile. His words were his acknowledgment of what might have been if either of them were different people. Her soft good-bye floated gently on the breeze between them. The last thing she saw as she guided the van into the quiet street was him watching her drive out of sight.

5

What an evening! Jenny stared blankly at her bare feet where they were propped on the low table in front of the couch. She slumped dejectedly against the sofa cushions, fighting the urge to bury her face in their cool softness and give way to the tears welling in her eyes. It was impossible to feel so bereft because a man she hardly knew had kissed her and then said good-bye. But she did. Somehow, in a few short hours, he had become a part of her. He had touched her in a manner no human being had ever done.

A sob tore at her throat, echoing heartbreak in the silence. Jenny clenched her hands until the fingernails dug deep into her palms, leaving tiny deep-pink crescents. How had he reached her? Why had she opened herself to him, allowed him even the smallest glimpse of the person she really was? She had told him so little in words, yet he had read so much. She felt vulnerable, stripped bare of defenses.

Was she just one of those many women who fell victim to the practiced Masters' charm? Was that it? She could not, would not believe it of herself.

"No, no and *no!* I'm not going to sit here like a lovestruck teenager mooning over a man I barely know," Jenny vowed. "He's gone. And that's the way we both want it."

Casting off her melancholy, she straightened her spine and rose to her feet. She would erase him from her mind. Tomorrow was another long workday. With the ball coming up, she had more than enough to do. There were suppliers to contact for the extra inventory needed for the extensive decorations, not to mention the increased demand for floral tributes for the female guests. Jenny went to sleep with dreams filled with pink dogwood blossoms and roses, petite blond belles and lean, tawny-haired escorts.

Saturday was every bit as busy as Jenny had anticipated. She and Maggie hardly had time to speak to each other let alone have lunch together. By the time Jenny stumbled up the stairs to her apartment that evening, she was too weary to do more than tumble into bed. The following week remained the same, with both Jenny and her two assistants working flat out.

"Thank the good Lord it's Sunday tomorrow," Maggie groaned as she sank into the chair near Jenny's work table. She wiggled her feet out of her shoes and propped them against the rungs of Jenny's stool. "I feel like I'm a million years old."

Jenny slid off her perch and stretched tiredly, one hand rubbing the base of her spine in a slow massage to ease her aching muscles. "I know what you mean. I don't ever remember it being so busy this time of year. It reminds me of Christmas."

Maggie eyed her young employer with motherly concern. "I hope you're going to rest up for Monday. With the ball only a week away, you'll need your strength."

"Don't I know it! If I weren't so wiped out from the shop, I'd have nightmares about it." She sighed and relaxed into the other chair beside Maggie. "I spoke to Belle Fleur yesterday and they promised faithfully to have those extra daffodils I ordered added to my original request. I can't believe I made such an error in my calculations." She shook her head, remembering her dismay when she realized she had underestimated the number of potted flowers she needed by fifty containers.

"Frankly, I don't know how you managed to keep up with everything. By the way, have you called Jim Nichols back yet?"

"No, I haven't had time."

"Well, make time, girl. He's sure to ask to take you to the ball." Realizing what she had let slip, Maggie's eyes rounded in horror before she shut them briefly.

"What have you done?" Jenny asked in a carefully neutral tone. "Maggie?" she prompted when her friend didn't answer immediately.

Faded blue eyes held an abashed apology as they met Jenny's determined gray stare. "I . . . uh . . . mentioned you were going to attend this year."

"And?" Jenny knew by Maggie's expression there was more.

"He wanted to know if you had a date, and I said no," she finished in a rush, expecting an explosion. And she got it.

"You did what!" Jenny's amazed question ended in a shriek of outrage. "How could you!"

Maggie folded her ample arms across her bosom and glared at her accuser sternly. "Now you just hold on. Jim is a nice man. He's got a good job, too. Eligible *and* attractive college professors don't grow on trees, you know."

"Yes, but . . ." Jenny began, hoping to stem the

glowing list of qualities of one of her more persistent suitors. She freely admitted she liked the quiet, sandy-haired teacher better than most of the males she had dated. He was just so serious. He never really laughed at anything.

"No buts. You need someone to go to the gala with and he wants to take you. Nobody is askin' any more than that."

"All right." Jenny threw up her hands in surrender. "I'll think about it."

"You'll call him," Maggie persisted.

Exasperated, Jenny shrugged irritably. "Maybe."

Maggie's face softened slightly, her lips curving into a smile. "You know you'll enjoy it more if you have an escort for the evening."

Sunday came and went without Jenny picking up the phone to return Jim's call. While she knew Maggie was correct about the fact that she'd feel better with a date, she wasn't sure if Jim was the one she wanted—not that there was a lot of choice. She certainly didn't have a string of men waiting around for her to call them.

Monday afternoon found her no closer to a solution as she headed for the country club to check on the measurements for the small floral grotto Mrs. Masters wanted constructed in the gardens. The morning had been busy but not hectic; she was thankful, since she needed the delivery van. She really ought to see about getting a car of her own. With her business expanding the way it was, she couldn't keep using the truck. For one thing, it was almost never free. Besides, it presented a better social image for her elite clientele if she had a nice little car.

Smiling at the pleasant thought, Jenny turned the blunt-nosed truck into the country club's stately curved driveway with sentinel oaks guarding the entrance. She hummed happily to herself as she slipped through the side door to the terrace and the gardens. The sight of Daniel's sleek head bent attentively over the petite Cynthia instantly killed her mood.

She had been so rushed since she had last seen him, she hadn't had time to think or remember. Now, faced with his presence, she was stunned at the memories flooding her mind. Motionless, she stared at the golden couple, her ears easily picking up their conversation.

"You decide, dahling. I simply can't make up my mind," the lovely blonde pouted.

Daniel's smile was indulgent as his eyes rested on her upturned face. "The pink, I think," he murmured.

Jenny watched Cynthia raise on her tiptoes and press a kiss against Daniel's tanned cheek. "You always know what's best for me." The woman leaned against his shoulder for a moment. "Will you wait here while I see the manager for Edna? I'll be right back, sugah."

Jenny felt a surprising urge to gag at the saccharine sound of Cynthia's dulcet voice. How could Daniel tolerate such a woman, she wondered in disgust? She studied the lean supple body, admiring his athletic build. When her gaze finally reached his face, she found herself looking straight into his brilliant eyes. There was a smile of welcome there and a brief flare of something more. It was gone in an instant.

Daniel strolled toward her, his expression one of a friend meeting a friend. "What brings you here, Jenny?" he asked, one tawny brow arched inquisitively.

Stifling the surge of emotion flooding her at this unexpected encounter, Jenny descended the terrace steps. She was grateful for the years of practice she had had at hiding her feelings. It enabled her to return his smile almost naturally. "I needed some more measurements," she explained when she stopped beside him. "And you?" she tacked on, hoping to convey the impression she had just arrived. Some instinct told her not to mention Cynthia.

Daniel hesitated for a split second before he answered. "I brought a friend of mine on an errand about the ball."

Jenny exhaled slowly, surprised to find she had been holding her breath. For a moment there, she had thought he would lie. Not that she had any right to question him, or he to answer. She should've known better—hadn't he proved his honesty to her beyond all doubt? "I saw her. She's very pretty," Jenny commented quietly.

Daniel's shrewd eyes probed her calm face seeing behind the serene mask. "She is. It's part of the requirements," he replied, knowing exactly what Jenny was *not* saying.

Jenny gasped at the blunt assessment. "That wasn't kind," she chided. Then spoiled it with a giggle. Magically the sick feeling in the pit of her stomach vanished at Daniel's easy dismissal of the blonde's charms. "I don't think Cynthia has much in common with Lilly. I can't see her tramping through the woods at dawn—"

Jenny didn't get a chance to finish her thought before Daniel took her arm, giving her a warning look. "Save it. We've got company." He tipped his head slightly toward a couple emerging from the hallway, and pulled her down the marked path toward the gardens.

"Where are we going?" Jenny demanded, tugging ineffectually at the viselike grip on her elbow.

Daniel didn't pause in his stride. "Out of earshot of

the club." Reaching his destination, he pushed Jenny down on a secluded white wrought-iron bench and sat down beside her.

"You can let go of me now," Jenny said sweetly, her eyes glinting with annoyance over his treatment. When he released his hold, she massaged the spot, glaring balefully at him. "I bruise easily, you know."

"You're crazy, do you know that?" Daniel commented grimly. "I've never met such a woman for getting into messes in my life. In another minute you would've told the whole world how you let Lilly trick you."

She felt the irritation in him, but ignored it. "Trick me?" The last word was a squeak of indignation.

"That's what I said. If that story gets around, you know damned well your business will suffer," he shot back. His brows were drawn together in a frown at her obtuseness.

"You sure it's not your reputation you're worried about?" Jenny flashed, then bit her lip at the nasty accusation. What had gotten into her? Not only had Daniel been more than understanding about her part in Lilly's theatrical gesture, but he had also refrained from getting his own back. And he could've very easily, she acknowledged critically. She ought to be grateful for his attitude instead of attacking him.

"Now who's not being kind?" Daniel mocked.

"I'm sorry," she offered apologetically. "I shouldn't have said that." She paused for a second. "You're right, of course. I shouldn't have brought up Miss Tyler either. It's none of my business, especially after the way I behaved." Her lips curved in a rueful smile. "Could you ignore that last bit and put it down to a thoroughly crazy week?"

Daniel's expression lightened at her explanation, the tension in him ebbing slightly. "That bad, hmm?" he asked, eyes glittering with amusement.

Jenny nodded. "Yes," she sighed. "There's a million things to do to get ready for the ball."

He lifted one strong, tanned hand to trail his fingers against Jenny's cheek, the humor fading from his eyes. "You do look a little tired," he murmured softly.

Jenny's lashes fluttered shut as she savored the tingling warmth of his gentle caress. She ached to turn her lips into the questing hand, but she forced herself to remain still. He had made it clear he would seek nothing from her, in spite of the attraction between them.

"I wish we hadn't met today." He searched Jenny's upturned face, the dark fans of lashes lying against the pearly skin. His eyes lingered on the rich curve of her lips. He dropped his hand to his side. "Or maybe I wish you didn't have those dreams of yours," he whispered quietly.

Jenny opened her eyes at the almost inaudible words. In that second, she too wanted to be free of her need for a home, a family and a man to spend her life with. She longed to take whatever happiness Daniel offered. But she couldn't; she had spent too many years deprived of a place of her own to give up her hopes of belonging to someone, of being wanted, of being loved. Smoky clouds of regret conveyed her feelings to Daniel's perceptive eyes more eloquently than words ever could.

"I'd better get back." The flat statement carried Daniel's acceptance and his understanding.

Jenny stood up, her face a calm mask to hide the sorrow filling her. "And I should get a move on. Maggie will be wondering where I am." She turned to take the path leading away from the clubhouse and Daniel.

"Good-bye again, Jenny Brown."

Jenny hesitated midstride. The deep-throated caress of Daniel's simple leave-taking almost cracked her resolve. It took all her will to keep on walking without looking back. With each meeting, it was harder to hold on to her plan for the future.

Mechanically, Jennifer found and measured the area designated for Edna Masters' pet project. There was no sign of Daniel or his blond companion when she skirted the terrace, choosing the outdoor path to the parking lot. She didn't feel up to coping with Daniel's latest flirt. It wasn't jealousy as much as it was the fact that she couldn't be a part of his life. She needed a commitment, and Daniel would not or could not give her one.

She was on her way back to the shop when his attitude suddenly struck her as odd. Why did he refuse any close ties with a woman? And why did he respect her own determination to have marriage or nothing? With the attraction between them, surely his natural reaction should have been to pursue it. But he hadn't. While openly admitting his response, he had backed off. Jenny's eyes narrowed thoughtfully. Why? the practical side of her demanded. On the surface, he sounded an improbable knight in shining armor, wishing only his lady's happiness. But in this day and age! No way! Even in the slow-paced south, chivalry was a dying life-style. Was he afraid of deep emotion? She shook her head at the thought. His behavior was a puzzle with no answer.

Jenny parked the van behind the shop and hopped out. One thing for sure, she wasn't going to the ball alone. She would call Jim tonight.

"Good grief, girl, who got you so mad?" Maggie asked in surprise as she looked up and saw Jenny come in.

"No one. Why?" she replied, bewilderment chas-

85

ing the frown from her face. She hung the truck keys on the hook beside her workbench, then slipped her arms into her smock.

"You looked so fierce . . ." Maggie's voice trailed off suggestively, inviting Jenny's explanation.

Jenny glanced over her shoulder, pausing in her search through her phone index for Jim's number. "I was thinking about Saturday night," she murmured briefly before resuming her hunt. "There it is," she exclaimed triumphantly.

Perching on her stool, she dialed Jim's college office, waiting impatiently for him to answer. She knew Maggie was surprised at her behavior, but she ignored her for the moment. This was the first time in her life she had called a man for a date. She wanted to get it over with before she lost her nerve.

Jim made it easy for her. "I was just about to phone you, Jen," he exclaimed when he heard her voice.

"Oh."

"Maggie mentioned you were going to the Dogwood Ball this year. If you haven't already made plans, I was hoping you would let me escort you."

The hesitant tone in Jim's gentle voice made Jenny feel guilty about accepting his offer. Jim had made it clear he wanted to be more in her life than just a casual date. He was attractive, had a good job, was kind and very considerate. In short, he had all the qualities one looked for in a lifelong mate. But she didn't love him. Try as she might, she could only care for him as a good friend.

"Jenny, are you still there?"

Startled out of her reverie by the anxious voice in her ear, Jenny marshaled her thoughts. "Yes, Jim, I'm here." She paused a second to take a quick breath. "And I'd be pleased to go to the gala with you," she agreed in a rush.

"Great!" he enthused, sounding delighted. "What time do I pick you up? You'll need to be there early, won't you? And what color is your dress? A florist can't possibly go without special flowers of her own."

Smiling slightly at the eager note in Jim's voice, Jenny gave him the information he sought. His obvious desire for her company dispelled some of the ache within her over Daniel's absence.

"Well, finally you're showin' some sense," Maggie remarked with satisfaction when Jenny hung up the phone.

"What?" Jenny turned to her friend.

"I said I'm glad you took my advice," Maggie repeated, a curious look on her face. "I just don't understand why you were in such an all-fired rush to call?" She paused expectantly.

Jennifer shrugged evasively, not ready to admit the strange emptiness inside her demanding relief. "It suddenly dawned on me I had forgotten to call Jim. That's all."

Jenny didn't know whether or not Maggie believed her. She hoped she did, for she didn't wish to hurt Maggie's feelings. How could she possibly tell Maggie she had just accepted Jim because she couldn't have Daniel? It was too unbelievable for words. Maggie wouldn't understand in a million years. She wasn't even sure she did herself. She was groping in a maze of conflicting emotions, fighting the dictates of her head and the inclinations of her heart. The future had never been so obscure. It was like those black days of her early childhood and the endless succession of foster families. Her security was in jeopardy. Now, as then, she had to fight back. The difference was, she was her own enemy. Jim was her shield. She had to exorcise this demon of desire that turned her body to molten honey and her heart to a wild thing whenever Daniel was near.

Daniel had made it clear he would not be the one to tamper with her dreams. But if her visions of the future were altered, or didn't exist, what then?

The simple truth was, Jenny no longer trusted herself.

That unpalatable fact stayed etched in her mind as the ball loomed ever closer. In spite of the frantic pace she set to get everything ready on time, she couldn't shake the secret fear invading her very soul. She hated the way she unconsciously sought Daniel's lean form each time she entered the country club, especially the gardens. She wanted to banish his image from her mind, yet the harder she tried, the more firmly entrenched he became.

Saturday morning dawned bright and clear. Jenny opened one reluctant eye to locate the stridently ringing bedside alarm.

"Five forty-five," she groaned, a bare arm emerging from the tangled sheets to slap at the clock, stilling the shrill clamor in mid buzz. Pushing aside the pale peach covers, Jenny got up. The soft blush of the early morning sun cast a pink glow over the cool bedroom and the stunningly unadorned Jenny. What Jenny lacked in conventional prettiness, she made up for in figure.

From the top of her delicate head with its lovely layered tresses to the slender arches of her surprisingly small feet, she was a vibrant young goddess. Firm, high-tipped breasts rose proudly above a tiny waist. Long, graceful legs flowed from deliciously curved hips. And her walk! The smooth stride combined with an unconsciously provocative sway was a lyrical sweep of sensuality. In the form of Eve she was a temptress of ancient lore, as innocent of her power as the first woman in the Garden, and to be just as lethal to the man of her choice.

Padding silently to her bath, Jenny was unaware of

her potential. Her tired mind knew only one fact. In a few short hours, all her preparations, all her work would become a reality. Success or failure? Each year it was the same. The nervous energy, the worry and the struggle to make this year's ball better than the one before.

Her eyes were gritty with fatigue as she stepped under a cool shower. Her moan of protest of the deliberately icy temperature was clearly audible. Much as she hated cold showers, it was one sure way of waking up.

It had been well after eleven last night when she had put the finishing touches on the centerpieces for the buffet tables. If it hadn't been for Billy's older sister, Josie, and Maggie, she might not have gotten any sleep at all. Between the two of them, they had transferred Jenny's ideas for the grotto into a reality of chicken-wire panels covered with lush ferns, yellow mums and white carnations. Now all that remained was transporting her floral creations to the club.

Keeping one eye on the clock, Jenny dried quickly and slipped into her jeans and smock. Billy, Maggie and Josie were due at 6:30. Josie was to help Maggie prepare the corsages ordered for the event. With the extra help, Jenny and Billy were free to devote their time to the decoration of the ballroom.

She started down the stairs to the shop, hearing the deep-throated growl of Billy's supercharged Ford as it made the turn at the end of the street. She checked her watch before opening the back door of the store. Immediately her nose twitched, inhaling the delicate scent of the sea of golden yellow blossoms inside the workroom. Everywhere she looked there were flowers. The cases were filled and overflowing in the shop itself, and every available counter and inch of floor was alive with color. The narrow walkway leading from the back door to the front of the store was just wide enough for careful passage.

"Right on time, Jenny," Billy announced with a grin as he slid out of his fire-engine-red car, the pride of his young life. He was followed by his two female passengers, Maggie and Josie.

Jenny grimaced in response to his early morning exuberance. "I'm glad this is a business area. If I lived in a regular neighborhood, I'd be in real trouble with all the racket you're making."

"Just be happy you didn't hitch a ride in that contraption," Maggie added teasingly.

"Mom's threatened to lock him out of the house if he doesn't get a new muffler." Josie's eyes twinkled engagingly at her younger brother.

"Ah, come on, girls, lay off," Billy complained. He pointed toward the open door. "I thought ya'll wanted to get started."

"Hark him, the slave master," Josie chortled. She peered in the back room. "I was hoping some nice little elves had come in overnight and finished up for us."

"'Fraid not," Jenny responded. She gestured toward the potted plants. "Let's load these first."

"That's the last of the crocus and daffs. Do you want me to start on the grotto sections next?"

Jenny stood up, stretching her aching back muscles gingerly. Her eyes swept over the lush golden bordered orchestra dias with satisfaction before turning to Billy. "Not yet. I want to leave those in the refrigerator as long as possible. Bring the tubs of dogwood and the ferns next, I think, and the centerpieces, if there's room."

With a nod, Billy departed, leaving Jenny alone once more.

"We meet again, Jenny Brown."

Startled at the quiet greeting, Jenny whirled around, making contact with a solid chest. Off balance, she instinctively clung to Daniel, and for a moment her body melted into the hard length of his. She felt his arms tighten around her as she raised her eyes to his face. "Do you always sneak up . . ." The rest of her sentence died when she saw the desire kindled in the brilliant blue depths. She couldn't speak, let alone move. Her eyes traced his features, lingering on the mobile lips just inches away. She ached for the pleasure, the fire that only they could ignite. She watched mesmerized as they curved into a smile.

"Do you know what you're asking, my girl?" Daniel murmured whimsically.

A delicate flush stained her cheeks as she realized the direction of her thoughts. Suddenly aware of her position, she stiffened in his arms. "You can let me go now," she whispered.

His arms stayed locked around her slender form. "No reward for saving you?"

Jenny shook her head, her gaze fastened on the knot in the conservative blue tie. Every nerve in her body was alive to Daniel's potent masculinity. She would like nothing better than to relax against him, but she dared not. She felt his sigh as her own, and then the slow, almost reluctant easing of his embrace.

She took two steps back, feeling immeasurably relieved at even that small a distance between them. It was increasingly clear that she had little willpower where he was concerned. And as time went on, it was becoming more difficult, not easier, to deny the attraction she felt for him.

"What brings you here this morning?" she asked in an effort to restore some semblance of normality.

"Edna needed to check on the final details for

tonight. Since I go right past here on my way downtown, I offered to do it for her." He glanced around the ballroom. "I don't need to ask why you're here. It looks even better than last year."

Jenny followed his eyes. "I hope so. It's so hard to give your best each year, then go out and try to top yourself the next." She sighed. "Now if the grotto just holds together, I may survive one more gala."

"Grotto?" One tawny brow quirked in amusement over glittering blue eyes. "Let me guess: my mother."

Jenny grinned at the resigned, knowing tone in his voice. "Actually, it was a stroke of genius, as ideas go."

"But?" he questioned curiously, sensing something in her answer.

"The dimensions were a bit of a problem," she confessed. "It had to be wide enough for two to sit down comfortably and high enough to avoid decapitating some unsuspecting male in the middle of a romantic interlude."

Daniel's husky laugh rippled along Jenny's nerve endings, kindling a response deep within her being. "That would be a bit awkward," he agreed. "I'll offer myself as a test case if you want to try it out."

The intriguing notion of Daniel beside her in the scented grotto conjured up need within her so strong she was unable to suppress a murmur of longing. Her eyes deepened to smoke as she stared at him.

He leaned toward her, searching her expressive face.

Jenny swayed closer, caught in the spell he wove, unable to deny the power he had over her. When his arms closed around her pliant body, Jenny sighed deep in her throat, a purr of satisfaction more provocative than she knew. Daniel's mouth closed over hers, swallowing the seductive feminine sign of surrender as he feasted on the honeyed lips she offered him. His tongue probed delicately at the deepest recesses of her mouth, igniting a slow fire of passion between them. His arms tightened, seeking to absorb the very essence of the woman he held. Caught in a blaze of increasing need, Jenny arched against him, demanding all of him.

"Mr. Masters?" The questioning inflection of an alien third voice close by shattered the mood like a shower of icy rain.

Jenny drew back sharply, her breath coming in ragged gasps, aware as never before how close she was to the edge of betraying herself irretrievably. Thank whatever fates that be, they were s,hielded from the view of anyone entering the main doors by the orchestra stage. The last thing she needed was to be found in the Masters heir's embrace by one of the club's staff. She shuddered at the thought.

"Are you all right?" Daniel asked in a low, husky voice. He raked a hand through his ruffled hair as he sought to control his breathing.

Jenny nodded, making an effort to dampen the unfulfilled longing she knew her eyes betrayed. Nothing had changed for either of them. "You'd better answer him before he starts looking for you," she murmured quietly.

"Jenny, we need to—" Whatever he intended to say was interrupted by the repeated calling of his name, accompanied by nearing footsteps. "Damn," he muttered before stepping briskly into the open to confront the unknown person. "Yes, Thornton, what is it?"

Jenny leaned weakly against a supporting column, hearing the barely restrained impatience in Daniel's curt question. Another minute and she would have been caught in a very embarrassing position. What had come over her, she wondered bleakly as she listened to the pair of retreating footsteps that told her that Daniel had taken the inquisitive Thornton and left. How could she keep responding to this man every time he waltzed into her life? He said he wanted no part of her, yet he kissed her over and over again. Was this some new game dreamed up by the rich when more common pleasures failed to soothe jaded palates? The thought sent a shaft of pain piercing to her very heart.

She paled as the possibility took hold in her chaotic mind. In a twisted way, the facts supported her. After all, a man with Daniel's experience knew enough about women to judge her response, how best to achieve what he desired. And what he desired was her, of that she had no doubt. Only one thing stood between him and his objective. Her dreams! Her brain whirled with the implications.

He had known exactly how to reach her, this golden-haired stranger with the gift of reading her mind. How simple and incredibly naïve she had been. Now she understood the seemingly reluctant attraction, the apparent honest refusal to hurt her by destroying her visions for the future. Strategy, pure and uncomplicated. The teasing intimacies, the hardened rake trying to respect a woman's scruples. That was the biggest laugh of all, she acknowledged gulping back a sob. She blinked angrily at the stinging moisture in her eyes. She cringed at the thought of facing him tonight. More than ever she was thankful for the shielding presence of Jim. At least she was spared the humiliation of appearing unescorted.

Mentally aching and physically exhausted, Jenny still managed to create a fantasy of yellow and gold for the highlight of the Dogwood Festival.

* * *

As she entered on Jim's arm shortly before the ball officially started, she gazed around the glorious ballroom with critically objective eyes.

The band was in place and tuning up, their dull gold jackets and dark brown pants a perfect foil for the vibrant border of yellow daffodils. The twin dogwoods with their snowy white blossoms stood guard at the main entrance providing the theme for the ball. Pale primrose linens graced each of the small tables grouped conveniently about the sumptuous room. There was a long buffet table running the length of a smaller dining room off the dancing area. The vivid splash of golds, yellows and ambers were caught and reflected in the elegant crystal and gleaming silver of the elaborate feast. The crowning touch was an exquisite ice sculpture of a spray of dogwood blooms.

"Honey, you outdid yourself this year," Jim commented warmly against her ear.

Forcing a smile to her lips in response to his sincere praise, Jenny slanted a glance at her companion. How good-looking he was, she decided with an outsider's view. Why was it she could feel nothing but ordinary fondness for this man? She knew the most impassioned kiss from his lips wouldn't stir her the way a touch of Daniel's hand did. He deserved more than she could give him.

"How would you know?" she teased in a deliberate attempt to enter into a festive mood. She would not spoil this evening for him. She owed him that much at least.

He grinned, his gentle gaze fixed on Jenny's face. "I saw the pictures you took from the last ball, remember?" His hand exerted a light pressure on Jenny's arm. "Now, how about showing me this grotto you designed."

Jenny was more than willing to comply with his request, glad to escape the ballroom for even a limited time. With any luck, Daniel and his entourage would arrive before they returned. Once the guests made their appearance, she knew it would be easier to escape his notice, since it was his practice to play host at his mother's gala.

"This is really something, Jenny," Jim enthused when he halted once again at her side, after he had circled the fragrant alcove, noting the carefully hidden supports and tie wires holding it in place.

Jenny laughed, a light silvery sound of pleasure at his unstinting praise. "You're so good for my ego," she teased, half seriously.

She glanced around the romantically lit gardens, enjoying the feel of the soft spring breeze on her skin. The drifting sounds of slow melody filled the air. It was truly a beautiful setting, Jenny admitted honestly —if only she could forget the man who waited inside.

The sprinkling of conversation she detected coming from the terrace indicated the guests were arriving. Her nerves tightened as she realized she must leave the safe seclusion of this natural wonderland. She had to go back.

"Jenny?"

Startled out of her thoughts by the touch of Jim's warm hand on her bare arm, Jenny turned faintly haunted eyes to his face.

"Hey, what is it?" he asked in concern, seeing her expression.

Jenny lowered her lashes for a second, gathering herself. She had never realized what a coward she was until now. The idea of watching Daniel pay court to the beautiful Cynthia was sheer torture. Shaking her head, she managed a slight smile. "Nothing," she denied, lifting her lashes. "I was wondering if this dress was a bit too revealing." The lie came easily to her lips, and Jim accepted it without question.

"You're beautiful to me no matter what you wear," Jim murmured in a suddenly intense whisper. He gazed raptly at Jenny's slender figure, silhouetted against the flower backdrop.

Jenny's gown was a deceptively simple wrap dress with a side waist closing. The deep V-neck of the halter-style bodice revealed a hint of pale satiny breasts above the silvery green silk bodice. The hem curved from a knee-high drape in front to a floor-sweeping point at her heels. The light fabric clung to her figure with loving strands discreetly highlighting her assets without being blatantly sexy. Slender silver loops hung from each tiny ear, lending an elegant sophistication to the layered cinnamon tresses. With the unusual light touch of silver and green eyeshadow to the thickly lashed gray eyes and the kissable blush of pearlized pink to her lips, she was a stunning picture of innocence and sensual appeal, as intoxicating as the finest wine to her susceptible escort.

"Jenny?" Jim's hands touched her shoulders, his fingers caressing the ivory curves almost reverently.

Jenny should have been prepared for the desire she saw flicker to life in Jim's hazel eyes. But she wasn't. Momentary surprise made her obey the light pressure of Jim's grasp as he drew her closer. The descent of his lips to hers stifled the protest she started to make. Unwilling to hurt his feelings by resisting him, Jenny stood quietly in his arms, feeling the carefully restrained hunger in him, yet unable to respond to it. Apparently her lack of reaction got through to him, for his lips ceased their searching.

Jim raised his head slightly to stare into Jenny's eyes. "It's not there, is it? I'd hoped if I gave you enough time . . ." His voice trailed sadly to a stop. He scanned her expressive features, seeing the understanding and the compassion in her eyes.

"I'm sorry, Jim." Jenny shook her head helplessly, hating the pain she knew her words were causing him. "If I could order my heart to love you, I would. There's a gentleness about you I've never known in anyone else." She sighed, and stepped out of his loosened embrace. "This evening was a mistake for us both."

"Don't say that," Jim pleaded quickly. "The evening should be a triumph for you. Don't let my poor judgment spoil it." He managed a creditable grin. "It's not as if you've ever given me any encouragement." He took her arm, his touch once again that of a friend. "Let's go join the party."

Jenny had no option but to agree. Every particle of her being wanted to go home, but she couldn't bring herself to hurt Jim any more than she had by insisting they leave. She dreaded the thought of seeing Daniel more than ever. The confrontation with Jim had destroyed what little poise she had. She was aching with guilt over Jim, and desire for a love she could never have. Love? Dear God in heaven, where had that idea come from?

Eyes blank with horrified discovery, Jenny halted on the ballroom threshold. She stared unseeing across the gathering crowd of dancers on the glass smooth floor. Her ears were deaf to the romantic strains of the orchestra. She had loved him first with an impressionable teenage girl's fantasy. Over the years that youthful crush had grown undetected into a woman's passion shrouded in the remaining clouds of dreams. Knowing the man, the warmth of his touch and the keen perception of his mind had brought her fantasy to life, and with it the love she carried in her heart.

She loved Daniel. She trembled at the inevitability of the three simple words.

She was scarcely aware of the comforting warmth of Jim's arm as he gathered her close to his body. Her eyes sought and fastened on Daniel's lean, aristocratic figure, the tawny hair glinting like new-minted gold beneath the old-world chandelier.

At that precise moment Daniel looked up, the faintly bored smile on his face for the blonde on his arm fading.

A flash of elemental awareness arced across the dividing space. Jenny stood poised on the frightening brink of a cliff's edge. She felt the sweep of his narrowed gaze, which took in Jim's protective hold, as if it were a cold draft of air over her sensitive skin.

"Are you cold?"

Temporary vertigo stole what remained of Jenny's composure. She leaned weakly against her companion for a precious split second while she exerted her will to control the unnerving sensations assailing her. His visual caress evoked the memory of his last kiss, the way his body had fitted her curves, the way she had responded. . . .

That look seemed to Jenny's heightened senses to last eons instead of the reality of a few heartbeats. Daniel cast one last glance over her face, his eyes lingering on her lips, then he turned his attention to his petite companion.

6

Are you okay?" Jim's voice held real concern as he guided her unobtrusively to a chair at a nearby table.

Pulling herself together sharply, Jenny nodded. "Just tired. It's been a hectic week," she admitted evasively. Would this night ever end? she wondered desperately.

Jim took a seat beside her. "Would you like me to get you something to drink? Or maybe something to eat?"

A little peace, Jennifer wanted to shout. "No, just let me sit here for a moment. Last night was a bit late, and running around this morning . . ." she explained quietly, her obvious tiredness lending an element of truth to her statement. "While I'm getting my second wind, how about finishing that story you started in the car," she suggested, more to divert his attention than from any interest on her part.

Ignoring her request for the moment, Jim leaned slightly toward her. "We can leave, if you'd rather," he offered solicitously.

Jenny sighed in exasperation, only softening her expression at the hurt mirrored in Jim's kind eyes. "I'm fine, really."

Knowing her pride, Jim subsided reluctantly, a rueful grin twisting his lips. There was an apology in the hazel depths, though he wisely didn't voice it. "Well, Miranda wore this skin-tight skirt—you know, the kind where a woman can't take a decent step, let alone bend or stoop," he began, picking up the tale of his attractive architecture student and the field-study class.

Keeping her gaze fixed firmly on Jim's gentle face, Jenny allowed the soothing commentary to flow around her, giving her a chance to recover her equilibrium. Smiling perfunctorily at the appropriate places, she pretended an interest. In reality, Jim had only a small portion of her attention. Most of her energies were directed inward in an attempt to quell the clamoring senses threatening to erupt.

Her efforts were only partially successful. She was unable to avoid brief glimpses of Daniel and his lovely partner as they moved gracefully across the dance floor. Each vision reinforced the stupidity of her own presence. Why hadn't she realized the depth of her feelings sooner? Maybe then she would have been prepared for the weakness invading her limbs at the sight of the bright blond head brushing the shoulders of Daniel's expensive cream cashmere jacket. She lowered her eyes in self-disgust, the sound of Jim's voice providing a sort of security for her to cling to.

". . . and the thing ripped straight up one side from hem to waist. Luckily, one of the others had a poncho-type jacket on. The crazy female tossed it around her waist like a second skirt and went on with the tour," Jim concluded with a chuckle of masculine appreciation for the girl's nerve.

Having caught the last of the story, Jenny laughed in apparent amusement. She saw Jim's face glow happily at her forced enjoyment, believing it to be genuine. "Let's dance," she suggested impulsively, deciding to shake off her fears for the present. Anything was better than sitting there brooding like a lovesick teenager.

Jim rose with satisfying promptness, an eagerness he did nothing to hide. Dancing was a favorite pastime of his, one that Jenny shared. As she moved into his arms, her fingers rested lightly on the shoulder of his off-white jacket, and she felt the familiar sense of undemanding caring she had always known in his presence. She relaxed slightly, allowing her steps to match his. By devoting herself exclusively to Jim, much to his obvious delight, Jenny was able to ignore Daniel's disturbing presence.

Somehow she got through the next hours with all the appearances of a guest having a delightful time. She received numerous compliments on her creative talents from the many people she knew. Although she didn't travel in this social level, she had a wide circle of acquaintances there, since most of those present were customers of Garden of Eden.

"Shall we sit this one out?" Jim queried some time later. They were both breathless from a rather upbeat cha-cha.

Eyes sparkling with laughter at his comically hopeful face, Jenny agreed. "In here or outside?"

"Outside," he voted with an exaggerated sigh. He took her arm, leading her toward the cool terrace. "For a lady who looked on the verge of fainting at my feet earlier, you're remarkably energetic," he teased, as he gestured questioningly toward the garden path.

Nodding her agreement, Jenny strolled slowly at his side. "I couldn't let a little tiredness bar me from the social event of the year," she shot back.

"I'm glad," Jim stated with sincerity. He stopped

beside the white wrought-iron bench sheltered by slender weeping willows. "Shall we sit here for a while?"

Taking her place, Jenny gazed around the lush garden. The sky overhead was a black velvet canvas sprinkled with diamond stars. The gentle breeze from the river carried the scent of night-blooming jasmine and a fragrant array of early spring flowers. Beside her, Jim seemed content to savor the peaceful interlude too. The music from the ballroom was a muted melody, almost a dreamlike echo of a forgotten era. The sound of two male voices raised slightly in amicable disagreement intruded on the silence.

"There you are, Nichols. Just the man I was looking for," one of the pair exclaimed, stopping before them. "Donald tells me you took a group of students out to my site last week."

Nodding, Jim rose. "Dean Smithson," he greeted the older of the two first before turning his attention to the speaker. "Was there some problem, Mr. Belair?"

"No, no. It's just that one of the group of youngsters is my godchild," Belair answered immediately. "My wife's just returned this week and is rather anxious about the boy, you understand. I'd like you to come inside and meet her, set her mind at rest." He peered at the younger man. "It would help a great deal if you could have a word with her." He grinned conspiratorially. "You know women. Worry you to death if they're upset about something. She's been mumbling feminine intuition at me for the past two days."

Jenny stifled a giggle at the poor man's harassed expression. She had been silent until now, but seeing Jim's indecision about complying with the man's request made her speak.

"I don't mind, Jim. I'll just sit here until you get back." She smiled at the relief on all three faces.

"I won't be long," Jim murmured gratefully before accompanying the pair back to the club.

Left alone in the darkness, Jenny truly relaxed for the first time that evening. She closed her eyes, enjoying the solitude. A whisper of footsteps impinged on her mind, but she disregarded it.

"Hello, Jenny."

Startled by the deep mocking drawl, Jenny's lashes flew open. Daniel's lean body filled her vision, momentarily robbing her of speech.

"Who's your friend?" He reached for her left hand, staring first at it, then back at her. "What's he to you that you allow him to hang all over you like he's been doing?"

Puzzled by the leashed anger contained in his question, Jenny gazed at him in confusion. "What are you talking about?"

"I'm talking about that man—the one who has been at your side all evening," he bit out, his blue eyes alive with barely suppressed emotion.

Whatever Jenny had expected when she saw Daniel again, it had not been this. Why was he so mad? What *right* did he have to object to anything she chose to do? "I don't see what business it is of yours who my date is," she stated with indignant emphasis. "And for your information, Jim does *not* hang on me!"

"I don't know what you'd call it then," he replied, goaded by her answer. "This isn't a college necking dance."

Jenny paled at the crude comment. She opened her mouth to deliver a scathing indictment on his uncalled-for denunciations, but he gave her no chance to speak.

"I couldn't believe my eyes when I saw the two of

you together. Knowing you, I thought he had to be
your fiancé at the very least."

"Well, he's not," Jenny replied tartly, thoroughly
provoked at his unfair attack. "He's a friend, and a
damned good friend. Not that I need to explain my
relationships to you." The liquid softness of her eyes
slated over with gray ice as she glared at her accuser.
"I didn't notice much reticence on your part with the
'dahling' Cynthia," she drawled in mocking retaliation. "You don't see me accosting you about *her*."

Jenny's life had taught her to meet aggression with
an equal force of her own. Nothing had been handed
to her on a silver platter; she had had to fight for
everything she ever wanted. But when she won, she
won fairly, without trickery. She was honest in her
dealings and expected others to be, too. Daniel's
misjudgment had touched a sensitive nerve, causing
her to leap to defend herself.

Taken aback by the slashing counterattack, Daniel
went still, his blazing blue eyes watching her with
strange alertness. "Does it bother you?" he demanded, apparently abandoning the subject of Jim.

The perceptive question effectively doused the
flames of her temper. Self-betrayal loomed like an
unwanted spectre a hairbreadth away. In the split
second that elapsed, she realized she must answer
now. Any hesitation and she was lost. Daniel's
experience with women and their reactions gave him
an edge she couldn't hope to match. "Of course
not," she replied coolly, striving for just the right
touch of amusement to carry off her next lie. "That's
just the point. Neither of us have the right to dictate
to the other." She forced a smile to her lips. "I
thought we were friends, not lovers."

Daniel searched her outwardly calm expression,
seeking to probe behind the sudden wall he sensed
between them. "Even in friendship, a person can

experience jealousy," he said slowly as though putting half-formed thoughts into words.

It was a shot in the dark, Jenny assured herself, while at the same time wondering how to counter this new threat. She studied him covertly through the protective screening of half-lowered lashes. She felt like a novice duelist facing a master swordsman poised for the final deadly thrust. With a hard-won courage that typified her approach to life, Jenny faced his superior strength bravely, her slender body wary, ready for defensive measures at the slightest hint of danger. "If the rapport between the people involved is deep enough, jealousy is possible," she conceded, giving ground and protecting herself at one and the same time.

"And ours isn't?" One tawny brow climbed in an unspoken challenge for her to deny what lay between them.

Jenny spread her hands helplessly. This tack was unexpected. In fact, the whole scene was unreal.

"What do you want from me, Daniel?" she whispered in confusion. "You admit an attraction that you won't pursue. You kiss me, then you leave. You attack me when I spend time with another man . . ." She waited, searching his face for enlightenment. She could read nothing in the blank aristocratic features. It was like looking at a handsome mask. Whatever his thoughts, he was keeping them hidden from her.

"What do you want of me?" she demanded desperately for a second time. It was a plea torn from the very depths of her.

Miraculously, the smooth golden mask dissolved before her eyes. The twin blue flames bespoke desire, not anger.

"I want what you can't give." He saw the question

in her eyes. "I want you. No ties, no commitments, no one else in your life . . . or mine." He laughed harshly at the sudden panic she couldn't hide. "Don't worry. I told you before, I'm not that much of a womanizer."

He reached out to stroke her satiny cheek with a gentle finger, ignoring her instinctive shrinking away. "I want to lock you up in a cage so no one can see you or touch you but me," he whispered in a tone so deadly serious Jennifer knew he meant every possessive word. "Do you have any idea what it feels like when I see another man's hands on you?" In a flash, the gentle touch became a velvet grip on her throat. "It tears me apart. Me!" Cynicism, self-knowledge echoed in the last single word.

"Maybe I want you to be jealous of Cynthia, of any woman." He gripped her bare shoulders, dragging her close to him in an uncharacteristically jerky move. "I want the depth of passion I sense in you," he whispered with aching intensity. Then he blotted out the stars as he lowered his head to claim her lips.

Jenny's sound of outrage was totally muffled by the impact of Daniel's marauding mouth. His kiss branded her with fire and male dominance in no uncertain terms. Finesse, technique, seduction, all dissolved under the plundering need in him. He swept boldly into the dark warmth of her lips, a short, punishing foray demonstrating her own inferior strength.

Hating her helplessness in his steellike embrace, Jenny ceased her ineffectual struggles and used the only defense left to her: limp, passive resistance. She would not respond to him in anger.

"That's better," he murmured in husky approval. His mouth continued to move over hers, seeking out the corners. When she sought to turn her head aside, his teeth caught her tender lower lip and closed on it, holding her prisoner even as his hands caressed her bare back, arching her closer to him.

Wave after wave of sensation flooded her mind beneath his overwhelming onslaught. Her senses were alive to the male strength of his body against the feminine softness of hers. His cologne, the clean scent of him surrounded her with each breath she took.

"No!" she muttered fiercely, fighting her traitorous responses. "I won't let you do this to me!" She wedged her arms between their bodies, pushing away with all her strength, force born of desperate fear. "Let me go, Daniel." She had to escape. Where was Jim? she wondered frantically.

Daniel lifted his head at her last demanding cry and gazed at her in patent disbelief. "You're turning me away, just like that?"

"I am!" she retorted, aware of the bruised feeling of her mouth. *I'll bet no one has ever said no to him before,* she mused, watching him absorb her words. She resisted the impulse to rub her aching shoulders where his hands had bitten into her tender flesh. There would be marks tomorrow. Brands of his possession. The thought made her angry all over again and she lashed out, "Just go back to one of your little blondes and leave me alone!" Before she had finished speaking, she knew she had made a mistake. She wanted to call back her ugly comment, but one look at Daniel's taut face told her it would be futile to try.

"At least they're women, not some self-righteous little prude," he mocked with cruel unerring accuracy at her most vulnerable point.

Pain so intense it stole her breath slashed through Jenny's unguarded heart. Her face whitened and froze, encased in icy anguish. In a moment she would get up and leave this arrogant, merciless aristocrat. Her eyes, slate with the hurt he had inflicted, raked him. "Get out of my life!" It was a command. Each word tore through lips bruised by his touch.

"With pleasure, lady." He rose, standing over her like some avenging lord of old. It was a moment suspended in time as they gazed at each other across a chasm deepened by the damaging words between them. "Are you all right?" he asked on a note of grudging concern.

"I will be when you go," Jenny stated clearly, her hands locked together in her lap to keep them from shaking. She glanced down at her clenched fingers, unable to watch him leave for the final time. There was a whisper of movement, then she was alone. God, so alone.

She sat completely still concentrating on her breathing. Inhale. Exhale. Calmly. *I will not cry. Not here. Not now. Please, Jim, come to me. I need to go home.* Long moments passed, decades in length before she heard footsteps coming out of the darkness toward her.

"Jenny, what's wrong? Are you all right?" Jim's anxious question echoing Daniel's words nearly snapped the restraint Jenny held on her emotions.

"Too much party," she lied, lifting a wan, pale face to him. "Would you mind taking me home?"

He agreed immediately. "Lucky I picked up your shawl and purse from the table," he said as he placed a supporting arm under hers and helped her to her feet. "We'll go through the garden."

Jenny followed Jim's lead blindly, scarcely aware of the gentle flow of conversation he kept up as he put her into the car and drove her back to her apartment. All her energies were centered on controlling her heartbreak until she was alone. Despite her protests, Jim insisted on seeing her to her door, waiting only long enough to be sure she was locked securely in.

Jenny leaned wearily against the closed panel, staring blankly across her haven. Dear heaven, how did she survive this night, she wondered in silent despair. Of all the eligible men in the city, why did she have to meet Daniel? Fall in love with him? Where was her sanity? Her instinct for self-preservation?

A sob tore its way past the constricting lump of pain in her throat. Fool! Tears welled in her eyes and began to trickle in delicate silver streams down her pale cheeks. Slowly, like a woman grown years older, she pushed away from the door and headed for the bedroom.

Damn him to hell! Why couldn't he have stayed gone that first time? Why did he kiss her again and again? Why did she fall in love with him? Stupid question. What woman wouldn't succumb to his charm, the sensual appeal of his seductive expertise? Shudders racked her slender body as she crawled onto her bed, unmindful of the beautiful gown she wore. Curling on her side like a baby, she clutched a pillow to her stomach and buried her face in the plush softness. Hurting, she cried out her heartbreak for the future that would never be, and for the past she could not change.

When the storm of grief finally subsided, she lay spent amid the tangled bedspread, her dress a wrinkled mess and her pillow soaked with tears. Drained and empty beyond caring about anything, she stared at the darkened ceiling. For more than an hour, she lay unmoving, then she roused herself and made her way to the bathroom. Mechanically, she stripped, cleansed her face and teeth and stepped into the shower. Allowing the warm spray to cascade over her hair and body, she washed away the ravages of Daniel's anger and her own feelings. Heat penetrated her icy limbs, restoring some life to her emotionally battered body.

She felt marginally better when she padded barefoot to the kitchen wrapped in a thigh-length terry robe. The light by the front door was on, but otherwise the apartment was in darkness. For once, the cheerful, welcoming aura she strove for grated. The inky shadows fitted her mood perfectly. Using the tiny hood light on her counter top stove, Jenny heated water for instant coffee and then switched off the small illumination, plunging the room into darkness once more. Cupping her mug in her hand, she paced silently back to the living room and curled up, her feet tucked under her, on the corner of the living room couch. She took a sip from her cup, letting the steaming liquid ease down her throat. Her mind was curiously blank, registering neither pain nor emotion.

Suddenly an insistent buzz penetrated the deathly stillness. Jenny raised her head listlessly and gazed uncomprehendingly in the direction of the entrance foyer. A second impatient summons brought a frown to her face, yet she made no effort to move or to answer. The third long demand finally reached through the wall of apathy surrounding her. She stirred slowly to life. Leaving her half-empty mug on the coffee table, she crossed to the door. She vaguely realized the late hour, and caution surfaced. Her hand froze on the lock.

"Who is it?" she questioned in a husky voice bearing the lingering traces of recent tears.

"Open this door!" Daniel's command, even muffled by the thickness of the panel between them, demanded compliance.

She fumbled awkwardly with the catch until it finally gave. She barely had time to step back before

Daniel pushed open the door and was inside with it shut behind him. Jenny stared at him in silence, purposely avoiding his eyes. She couldn't bear any more anger from him, not now. With dazed surprise, she saw the single white rose grasped in one tanned hand. Why was he carrying a flower? Her gaze focused on the creamy petals, her florist mind recognizing a Jack Frost. It was very similar to the one she had given him that Friday night. Her eyes flew to his face, a faint hope flickering to life. Could it be a peace offering?

She caught her breath at the depth of tenderness reflected in his indigo eyes. Entrapped in the intensity of his visual embrace, she waited. He narrowed the distance between them, then lifted the single virgin bloom to her cheek. The light, sweet fragrance filled her senses as the velvet petals were drawn slowly along her jaw to her lips.

"I'm sorry," he whispered softly, his breath a warm fan of air across her forehead. "Will you forgive me? I had no right to attack you."

The simple gesture, the seductive caress of his deep drawl melted the numbing blankness. Her eyes darkened in response, reawakening her emotions as she searched his finely drawn features, the clean angles and planes. She wanted to throw herself into his arms. Instead she dropped her gaze to the symbol of his contrition and took the rose from him, cradling the blossom tenderly in the palms of both hands. She wanted to say so much, yet she couldn't find the words. She longed to tell him of her love, but she was afraid.

"Can't you look at me, Jenny?" Daniel asked gently. He raised her downcast face with a firm hand under her chin. "You've accepted my rose. Does that mean you forgive me?"

Forced to meet his probing eyes, Jenny could only

nod. Exposed to the full force of the sensual Masters charm, Jenny had no defense against the rising tide of sensation sweeping through her. Her emotional storm had left her weak and vulnerable. She swayed, lightheaded with fatigue and the devastating effect of Daniel's nearness.

Concern sharpened his eyes as Daniel caught her shoulders in a steadying grip. Suddenly he noticed the darkened apartment beyond the small pool of light in which they stood. He noted Jenny's pale face and shadowed gray eyes. "My God," he muttered as she leaned heavily against his shoulder. Scooping her up against his chest, he strode toward the dark shape of the living room sofa.

Jenny felt no surprise at his actions, only a rightness so deep she accepted it immediately. She rested her head against his neck, breathing in the rich male scent of him like a starving woman. The strength of the arms cradling her so securely was a haven she never wanted to leave. She made no protest when he settled on the couch with her in his lap. The surrounding darkness contributed to the unreal co-coonlike feeling.

"What have you done to yourself?" Daniel demanded with rough gentleness. One hand lifted the rose from her grasp and placed it on the end table. "If this is for me, I'm not worth it." He stroked her hair with light fingers.

Never had his voice sounded so good. There was an endearment in every word he said. Jenny loved him for it.

"To me you are." Four words, yet they held all the pent-up love Jenny had in her heart, the longing and the need for him. She raised her head from his shoulder. "I think I love you, Daniel. I don't know how it happened, but I do. I can't bear not being with you."

Daniel groaned, a mixture of her own pain and his defeat. "Jenny, what am I going to do with you. Woman . . . child . . . so wise and yet so naïve." He tucked an errant curl behind her ear in a possessively tender gesture.

Although his expression was hidden in the shadows, she could hear the deep emotion in his voice. She felt him shift, then the room was bathed in the soft glow of muted light. Her eyes questioned his action.

"We are going to talk," he stated firmly, easing her off his lap and onto the cushion beside him. He picked up her right hand, holding it carefully in his grasp. He stared at their entwined fingers for a long moment before he raised his eyes to her face.

Jenny could read nothing from his expression. It was as though he had wiped it clean. She was suddenly frightened at the blank golden mask. Was he going to let her down gently? Tell her those kisses were a mistake? That all she could ever be was a friend?

"I've fought this chemistry between us for so long. From that night you came to my office." He smiled slightly in memory. "You stood there so determined to explain, while your eyes showed your longing to run. And when you gave me the rose . . ." He paused, his grip tightening on her fingers. "I can't tell you how I felt." He lifted his head, staring straight into her expressive eyes. "In that moment, I wanted you more than I've ever desired anything in my life. I intended to have you, too." His lips twisted at the shock on Jenny's face at his blunt confession.

"Why didn't you?" she asked puzzled, remembering her uncontrolled response to his kiss.

"I couldn't. It's that simple. Call it a latent sense of morality, a streak of chivalry." He shrugged dismissively. "The names don't matter. We talked, really talked. Something I've never done with a woman." A baffled look crossed his face. "I could understand the struggle you had to get where you are. I could appreciate the value you placed on marriage and a home. I couldn't destroy those plans by seducing you, so I let you go."

Jenny knew she was now seeing a part of Daniel few people knew. It was a measure of his honesty that he chose to reveal this vulnerable, usually protected side. Jenny's love made her eager for every thought, every emotion he would share.

"But you didn't let me go?" she asked, curious.

Daniel sighed, his eyes lingering on her lips. "No, I couldn't seem to help myself. Every time I saw you, I wanted to hold you, to kiss you."

"And you did," Jenny finished for him.

"And I did," he echoed with wry self-mockery. "Then I called myself all kinds of a fool for my stupidity."

"Why is it stupid, Daniel?" Jenny hesitated, hating the question she had to ask. "Is it because of my background?" She lowered her lashes protectively, unable to face the possibility that that was the bar to their future.

There was a dead silence for a full second before Daniel reacted. His hand tightened painfully on hers as he shook it hard. "Don't you *ever* ask me that again, do you hear me?"

Startled by the anger in his bitten-off words, Jenny raised her head, tilting her chin defensively. "Well, I know damned well you aren't married, so there has to be a reason."

"There is," he snapped, dropping her hand in her lap. He leaned back against the cushions, staring across the room.

Jenny carefully flexed her numb fingers, her eyes never leaving his face. "Well?" she prompted when he didn't go on to explain.

"I've seen what love can do and I don't want any part of it," he stated baldly. "It can be possessive and smothering. It turned my mother into a parasite, clinging to the man she professed to idolize." Daniel paused for a moment to collect himself before continuing his tale in a low voice. "My parents were very much in love when they married. So much so they were a bit of an oddity in their group. They went everywhere together. Then my mother got pregnant. It was a bad time for her. Her muscles were weak, making carrying me to term very unlikely. To give them both credit, they wanted the child enough to sacrifice months of separation while my mother lay in bed and my father traveled. In those days, he had just started the business and it took long hours and a lot of out-of-town visits." He glanced at Jenny for the first time since he began his tale. "Maybe it was her condition, I don't know, but mother became jealous and demanding, needing to know where my father was every second."

Jenny was saddened at the picture he painted, yet she couldn't help wondering what it had to do with his own attitude.

"Then I was born. You'd think things would've returned to normal, but they didn't. Once begun, it seems my mother couldn't stop her unreasoning demands. She hounded my father if he so much as looked at another woman. Yet she loved him and he her. Do you know, I can still remember the fights they had." He grimaced. "She was even jealous of his interest in his own son. I went to boarding school from kindergarten so she could continue traveling with Dad. If I hadn't had the German measles so bad she was forced to stay home when I was twelve, she would've been traveling with him when he crashed. For a long time, I think she blamed me for being left alone.''

Jenny's eyes widened, realizing the meaning of his final statement. "She wanted to die with your father?" What kind of a woman would choose death, leaving behind a twelve-year-old child who needed her?

"She did," he confirmed flatly. "Do you see now why I don't want a commitment?"

"No, I don't, Daniel," Jenny argued. "Surely you know your mother was an extreme case. Love doesn't have to be like that."

"Doesn't it?" he echoed skeptically. "How easily you have forgotten 'our little talk' in the garden. And how good you felt when I finished with you."

Jenny paled at the sarcastic reminder.

His glittering eyes held the knowledge of her tears and the hurt he had inflicted. "I see you haven't. Do you want to face that over and over again? If I react like that now, what would happen later, after we were married? Like my mother, I don't share. The difference is, I know what I am. For years I've purposefully steered clear of anyone who stirred me more than superficially. But you, with your great big gray eyes and beautiful body, got to me. And, damn it, I can't fight it anymore." He swung around as though drawn by a force greater than himself. His arms reached for her, dragging her against his chest. "What am I going to do, Jenny? Tell me how to get out of this maze."

Jenny felt the defeat in him, the desire he made no effort to disguise. Womanlike, she responded to the male call for succor and comfort. Curling her slender arms around his shoulders, she nestled close to his chest, letting her forehead rest against his chin. She felt the rigid tenseness of his body as she fitted her curves to his.

"It hurt like hell when you accused me of playing around with Jim," she admitted on a soft sigh. "I won't deny it." She paused, searching for the words to express her feelings. Daniel's heart beat rhythmically under her cheek, somehow giving her the courage to go on. "But what destroyed me was the thought of never seeing you again, never knowing your touch." The sudden acceleration in the life-giving throb beneath her ear made her lift her head. "I want to be a part of *your life,* Daniel." She hoped the subtle emphasis she placed on her words would convey their meaning. She was afraid to make it any plainer. Rejection was no new feeling to her, but Daniel's denial was something she wouldn't be able to bear. She wanted him badly. She loved him too much to face tomorrow unless she made the effort to meet him halfway. She would rather risk her dreams than live with the nightmare of his absence.

Daniel stared searchingly into her upturned face. He saw the smoky clouds of desire in her eyes, the pearl-toned velvet skin waiting for his touch. His gaze lingered on the softly parted lips that seemed to beg for his kiss.

"Do you mean it? Do you know what you're saying?" he murmured in a husky drawl of awakening male need. "Be sure, because I may not be able to let you go if you change your mind. I can't promise not to be possessive and jealous, because around you I am. Can you live with that?"

The love Jenny felt for him shone in her eyes. "I can if you trust me."

"I do," he answered quickly, earnestly.

"Don't you know how much I've always wanted

118

someone of my own, someone who wanted me, only me, always?"

A flame flared to life in Daniel's eyes at her words. With a groan of desire and need, he captured her lips hungrily, fastening on hers in a carefully leashed passion. More than eager to taste the passion of the man she had chosen, Jenny willingly offered herself for his delectation.

Daniel's hand stroked down the curve of her shoulder to the open gap of the robe at her throat as he kissed her. His fingers trailed delicately over the ivory skin, dipping tantalizingly under the soft roughness of the confining terrycloth. Jenny moaned as flames licked her nerve endings in response to his touch. She arched closer, her lips parting to their fullest as she sought to absorb the very essence of Daniel.

A tremor shot through her when Daniel's hand cupped the passion-swollen roundness of her breast. He pushed her gently down on the couch, his body following her descent until they lay breast to chest, thigh to thigh.

"Sweet little orphan," he said huskily against her ear as his teeth toyed carefully with the lobe he had captured. "How much I've needed you, desired you."

"And I've wanted you," Jenny cried, her hands tugging fretfully at the jacket he wore. He had too many clothes on. She wanted to feel his skin against hers, not some piece of cloth.

"Slowly, sweetheart," he murmured as he eased up enough for her to help him out of his coat. His blue eyes, deep indigo with desire, surveyed her passion-flushed face and bared breasts. "We have all night."

Jenny shivered deliciously at the seductive promise of his voice. She passed her tongue over her swollen lips, liking the faint taste of him she found there.

Daniel groaned deep in his throat at her gesture, his hands going to the single knotted sash at her waist. With a flick of his wrist, he released the last remaining barrier to his view of her delectable body.

"You're exquisite," he breathed, drinking in the sight of her slender curves.

Jenny trembled with desire and a rising tide of urgency. Suddenly she couldn't bear the inches separating them. Wrapping her arms around his neck, she drew him down on her body, lovingly absorbing the weight of him, reveling in the male hardness pressing her into the couch. She slid her fingers into his hair as his mouth claimed hers with the full spectrum of his own desire.

He possessed her mouth, plunging deep into the dark moist depths, then his lips swept down her throat to the rounded mounds of satin skin and their rosebud peaks. The rough pelt of his tongue rasped over one, then the other, bringing each to full bloom.

Jenny writhed sensually under the assault, no longer thinking, just feeling, experiencing the fullness of his expertise. His hands traced the lines of her body, feathery chills of sensations across her stomach and to the triangle screening her womanhood.

"Daniel," she urged, arching her hips against the marauding hands. Was this love, she wondered? This burning need to scream and claw. She ached for the fulfillment that only he could give. "Daniel, please." It was a woman's plea for her lover, holding the essence of her power and her weakness.

Suddenly Daniel stiffened, reality sweeping away the storm he had created. This girl was innocent and totally unprepared for the possible results of their lovemaking. For the first time in his life, he knew a fierce desire to protect a woman . . . even if it was from himself he was shielding her.

"No, Jenny, wait," Daniel's harsh denial grated across Jenny's tender skin.

"Why?" she demanded in a devastated whisper of disbelief. Her glazed eyes focused on his face. His breath, like her own, was ragged, telling of his own arousal.

His hands stroked soothingly over her heated body while he cradled her against him. "Because I'm not prepared."

"Prepared?" she echoed in confusion.

"There are risks, Jenny," he explained on a sigh.

Jenny's mind reeled at the clinical comment. How could she have forgotten so vital an issue. Horror widened her eyes at the realization of how close they had come. She barely noticed Daniel gently pulling her robe back in place.

"It's all right, Jenny. Don't look so upset. Nothing happened." Daniel smoothed back the wispy curls across her forehead and brushed the anxious lines with his lips.

Tears stung her eyes at his tenderness. "Are you all right?" she inquired huskily.

He grinned at her hesitant question. "I've been better," he admitted, shifting to a sitting position and bringing her with him. He flicked the end of her nose with his forefinger. "Tomorrow's Sunday. Let's spend the day together?"

"Where?" Jenny asked bewildered at the sudden invitation. Her body was still recovering from his lovemaking and he was talking about a date.

"Cade's Cove."

"In the Smoky Mountains?"

"Sure, why not. A friend of mine boards some horses. We could take a picnic lunch." He saw the surprise on her face. "You can ride, can't you?"

Jenny nodded.

"Is it a date?" he prompted when she didn't answer. "I'll bring the wine and the food."

When she smiled her assent, Daniel swooped to capture her lips. His kiss was fleeting, but it vividly expressed his unsatisfied needs. Then he rose abruptly to his feet and collected his coat from the floor. "Be ready at eight." He shook back an immaculate white ruffled cuff to display a paper-thin gold watch. "That gives you exactly five hours to sleep and dress." He smiled at her caressingly. "And if you want to leave your bra at home, I won't tell anyone," he teased.

Jenny's cheeks blazed with fire at his intimate comment. "I may wear a straitjacket," she warned, wrinkling her nose impishly.

Daniel slung his jacket over his shoulder, and with a deep, full-throated male chuckle he headed for the door. He opened it and paused, his hand on the jam. "If you think that's going to stop me . . ." With a wicked grin at her expectant face, he stepped over the threshold, shutting the panel softly behind him.

For a full second Jenny sat immobile, half believing he was coming back. The faint thud of his footsteps on the stairs told her he wasn't.

"Darn him!" she muttered with the annoyance of someone who hadn't gotten the last word. "Serve him right if I did."

She grimaced ruefully in self-realization. Her body still tingled with longing and barely leashed desire. She would need more than a straitjacket if she wanted to survive unscathed a day in Daniel's company. Thank heaven, she didn't need that kind of protection anymore, she thought with a satisfied smile of recently acquired knowledge. She loved Daniel, and he knew it. Some time in the future, she would be his woman. Maybe not tomorrow, but soon.

The knowledge should have brought her guilt for having compromised her long-held beliefs. But it didn't. She was proud of her feelings, even of her place in Daniel's life. The care he showed her, the understanding he had of her deepest thoughts made it right. Surely, with the depth of mutual communication and feelings they shared, love for her must follow.

She hugged the hope to her heart as she turned out the lights and slipped into bed. As she drifted off to sleep, a smile touched her lips at the image of a mountain picnic and wine.

7

It was amazing what three hours' sleep, one cold shower and two black cups of coffee could do for exhaustion, Jenny marveled as she eased the last pan of brownies from the oven. She had never felt better or more rested in her life. It was a glorious day outside. She knew because she had greeted the sun when it rose. The golden dawn was a pale reflection of her own happiness. She smiled at the bold-faced kitchen clock. Only thirty more minutes and he would be at her door. Humming to the slow country ballad on her stereo, she upended the homemade dessert onto the cooling racks.

"I hope you like nuts and chocolate, Daniel," she mumbled as she slipped the two racks into the freezer for rapid cooling.

While she waited, she quickly cleaned up the kitchen. She had just finished icing the bars with her own sour cream and fudge frosting and had put the last square into the plastic storage container when the doorbell sounded.

Jenny hesitated for a fraction of a second, suddenly overwhelmingly aware of the step she was about to take. Once she opened that door, there was no going back. Daniel had the power to touch her as no one had ever done. He could give her a glimpse of heaven and in the end condemn her to a hell unlike anything she had ever known. Did she want to take that chance?

The second buzz, much longer than the first, brought a soft smile to her lips, chasing away the mists of doubt clouding her eyes. Yes, she did want that opportunity. Whatever she and Daniel had for each other deserved its chance for fruition. As with her plants, there was a time for everything, and this was hers.

With a new-found confidence in herself, Jenny opened the door with her smile still in place.

"I half expected to find you still asleep," Daniel greeted her. His eyes did a slow, appreciative sweep of her casually dressed form. "I like those jeans, by the way." A very masculine grin accompanied his comment on her well-fitting faded denims that were a close match to his own in style and color.

Warmed by his obvious approval, Jenny felt even more certain she had made the right decision. "We look like twins, you know?" she observed while she stepped back so he could enter.

Daniel flicked her nose teasingly as he passed. "I wouldn't say that!" he drawled.

"I meant the matching blue shirts," she retorted, shaking her head at his deliberate obtuseness. She gestured toward the sofa. "Would you like a cup of coffee before we go?"

"Only if I get one of those brownies I can smell with it." He made himself comfortable on the couch and eyed her surprised face with amusement, one brow quirked wickedly.

"How did you guess?" Jenny demanded. "I swear you must have a degree in mind-reading. I'll have you know that was supposed to be a surprise."

"Quit grumbling, woman, and bring me my coffee or I won't take you to the picnic," he warned.

Jenny was not overly impressed with his attitude. "Promises, promises," she said dismissively, heading for the kitchen. "Daniel—" His name ended in a shriek of startled surprise as Daniel caught her shoulders and spun her around to face him in one smooth motion. His lips captured hers before she had a chance to do more than register the hard length of him taking her off balance.

The touch of Daniel's mouth, swift and sure, caught her parted lips with hungry accuracy. His tongue stroked the moist inner surface, feasting on the rich sweetness of her mouth. His hands moved down her arms to her hips, pressing her intimately against his own lean torso.

From the first explosive contact, Jenny was lost. His kiss was the fuel for the slumbering embers of passion he had ignited a few hours before. Aching for his possession, Jenny denied him nothing, responding with an ardor equaling his own. Her arms wrapped around his neck as she followed the guiding of his hands, arching her supple form against him. She wanted him . . . needed him . . .

"You make me forget every good intention I ever had," Daniel murmured huskily against her ear. He traced the line of her jaw back to her lips with hungry kisses. "You taste of chocolate."

"It's the brownies. I had one before you came," Jenny mumbled distractedly, too intent on reaching for his tantalizing lips to pay much attention to her words.

"You're a good cook." His mouth closed on hers, stifling further conversation.

Whimpering with pleasure and a deepening need, Jenny drove her nails into Daniel's shoulders, kneading the hard muscles in a feline caress that brought a deep rumble of masculine desire to Daniel's throat. For one brief moment of ecstasy, the flame of mutual desire flared alive like wildfire.

Then, with a last-ditch effort at control, Daniel pulled away until only his hands retained contact with Jenny's quivering body. Drawing deep breaths, he steadied her until she could stand alone.

Between soft pants, Jenny gasped, "Don't you dare ask me if I'm all right."

"Well, are you?" There was concern in Daniel's voice. "You'd better button up," he commented, watching as she tried to restore some order to her dishevelled clothing.

Jenny glared at him, irritated at how calm he appeared while she looked like she had been dragged through a bush backwards. She knew he had been as affected as she. Half of her wished he hadn't drawn back, while the other half was glad he had. More than anything, she wished he didn't have such an inflammatory effect on her. With him around, her sanity went up in smoke. She had planned to be so cool—poised and composed. Hah!

Daniel grinned at her, then glanced at his watch. "Why don't you go repair whatever while I collect the brownies. We've wasted enough—"

"Wasted!" Jenny all but shrieked. "If you think I'm going with you after a crack like that—Ow!" Her threat ended in a sharp cry of shock as Daniel pushed her toward her bedroom with a not so gentle smack.

"Move, woman. Wine and picnic await."

Jenny found it was easier to allow the momentum to carry her in the direction Daniel had sent her than to argue. "And don't *touch* those brownies," she ordered over her shoulder.

A moment later, she surveyed her passion-flushed face in the mirror. The careful application of subtle gray shadow she had used to highlight her eyes had been effective when she had put it on earlier, but nothing like this. Her gray eyes sparkled with new depth and the heightened assurance of a woman who knew she was desired by the man she loved. Her lips didn't have a trace of lipstick. Not that it mattered. They were attractively swollen with a deep rose bloom from Daniel's possession.

"Hey, don't take all day," Daniel called from the living room.

"I'm coming." Placing the lipstick she didn't need in a side pocket, Jenny grabbed her comb and quickly smoothed her hair back into place. Turning, she found Daniel leaning against the door jam, the plastic container of brownies tucked under his arm. In his other hand, he held the last bite of one square.

"I thought I told you to leave those alone," she scolded, moving toward him. She stifled a giggle as he popped the remaining morsel in his mouth and then carefully licked the traces of frosting from each finger in turn.

He pushed away from his resting post and took her arm in a proprietary gesture. "How am I going to know if they're worth the trouble of bringing along if I don't taste them?" he pointed out reasonably.

Jenny paused at the front door and set the lock. "Well, are they?" she asked as she pulled the door shut.

Daniel bent his head, brushing a light teasing kiss to the corner of her mouth. "Not nearly as tasty as you," he breathed against her lips.

Jenny gazed into the vivid blue eyes glittering with devilment. Her own reflected her enjoyment of his lighthearted teasing. Bantering with him was addictive. Almost as much as touching him was. "Just for that I'll eat them all myself."

Daniel drew himself up in defense of the brownies he held. "Nag, nag. How are you planning—"

"Not nags, horses." Jenny interrupted sweetly, cutting off his tirade. "You did promise to take me riding sometime this week?" She dodged nimbly out of the way of Daniel's swatting hand.

"If you're going to make stupid puns, it will be you staying home, not the brownies." He leisurely followed her mountain-goat descent down the stairs.

Jenny stopped at his car, breathing deeply of the clear morning air. "I love Knoxville in the spring," she murmured quietly.

"Have you always lived here?" Daniel asked when he handed her into the car.

She nodded, waiting until he got in the driver's side to explain further. "I'm afraid you're looking at a girl who hasn't ever been as far away as Chattanooga."

"Don't apologize to me or to anyone for what you are, Jenny," Daniel ordered, starting the car.

Startled at his comment, Jenny slanted him a curious glance. "Was that what you think I was doing?"

"If you weren't, you were giving a damned good imitation. Just because you don't know who your parents are and you've lived in one city all your life doesn't mean you're any less important. The people who matter aren't going to judge you because you only finished high school, or whatever other silly ideas you have in that head of yours," he commented, anger at her hypersensitivity edging his voice. Although he understood her touchiness about her background, he hated the inadequate feelings he knew it gave her.

Strangely warmed by his anger, Jenny reached out to touch his hand resting on his thigh. "That's the nicest thing anyone has ever said to me," she said simply, the force of her emotions lending a husky throb to her voice.

Daniel's fingers tightened briefly on hers. "Jenny, what am I going to do with you," he murmured with gentle humor. He carried her hand to his lips, taking his eyes from the road ahead long enough to notice the effect his tender gesture had. "Now, no more serious talk. Not today," he ordered as he released her hand. "Tell me what you know about the Great Smoky Mountains."

Jenny wrinkled her nose impudently at the authoritative tone. "I know they're the boundary between North Carolina and Tennessee and they got their name from the smokelike haze that usually hangs over them."

"Mmmm?" Daniel prompted.

"There are some fourteen hundred kinds of flowering plants in the park and it is world renowned for its variety of flora. The coves have a variety of broadleaf trees. Along the crest, which rises approximately six thousand feet, there are conifer forests like those in Central Canada," she elaborated, swinging into her best lecturing style. "I forgot to mention there's a Spring Wildflower Pilgrimage starting in a few weeks. I give a tour for my girls every year when it opens."

"Girls?" Daniel queried, shooting her a curious look.

"I coach a girls' swim team for the Y," she offered in brief explanation.

"I didn't realize nature hikes were part of aquatic training." He paused, a thoughtful look on his face. "When do you find time for a social life? Between your business, the catering, the college courses and helping out with disadvantaged kids—"

"I never said my girls were disadvantaged," Jenny interrupted in defensive protest.

"They are though, aren't they?" The shrewd blue eyes made a quick survey of her guilty expression before returning to the interstate ahead.

"Hey, I thought we weren't going to be serious," Jenny objected, mentally withdrawing slightly.

Daniel's uncanny ability to read her thoughts and understand her actions was frightening in its accuracy. Essentially a private person, she was sensitive to the mental wavelength they seemed to share. In a way it was an invasion of the mind—her mind. While she admitted to an emotional attraction to this golden-haired male, she was not ready to open herself completely to him. That required a degree of trust her new feelings had not yet attained. It would be too easy to surrender to this man—a man who desired her, but hadn't yet said he loved her. A survival instinct warned her to go carefully. Physical surrender no longer held any fear for her. But total emotional surrender?

After a sharp glance at Jenny's suddenly composed profile, Daniel ceased his probing. Returning to the subject of their destination and its history, he told Jenny about the Land of the Great Smoke and of the Cherokee Indians who gave it its poetically descriptive name. He topped off his running commentary with a vivid portrayal of the famous Cherokee Indian drama, *Unto These Hills,* which he had seen at Cherokee, North Carolina, the year before.

"I didn't realize Cherokee was so close," Jenny commented idly as they entered the park's main gate.

"We're very lucky living in this part of the country," Daniel observed, his free hand gesturing eloquently toward the gray bouldered hills rising about

131

the winding road. On Jenny's side the pavement ran along the stone-pitted swirling stream of crystal clear mountain water. "I've tried living in other cities, but I always come back here."

Jenny nodded, knowing the feeling. She didn't need to travel to know this was home. The majestic peaks with their outlines softened by a thick forest mantle of new green swept across the horizon in mighty billows of rich earth. The mysterious blue-gray haze that gave the land its name clouded the valleys, reaching to the lofty peaks.

"It is beautiful," she agreed in an awed tone. Somehow, no matter how many times she had visited the Smokies, she had never lost the exhilaration she felt from her first trip.

Daniel smiled understandingly at her rapt expression. "Have you ever seen them from horseback?"

"No," Jenny grinned. "My riding is strictly the walk-and-bouncing-trot variety. In fact, I don't know how I let you talk me into this."

"I'd like to think it's because you trust me not to let you get hurt," he suggested significantly.

Jenny heard the underlying question in his words. For a moment, she considered his statement. Did she trust him with her physical well-being? She had to admit she did. Her eager response to his lovemaking should have told her that, if nothing else. By rights she should be worried about committing herself to a man she barely knew. But she hadn't been—not on a physical level.

Not ready yet to carry her self-examination any further, Jenny resorted to answering Daniel's words minus the hidden demands.

"I trust you not to let me get hurt on a runaway horse," she admitted.

"That's a start, anyway," he murmured quietly as

the road in front of them opened into the wide, lush, green valley known as Cade's Cove.

Jenny glanced appreciatively around the gently sloped terrain. The sunlight danced along the fringe of trees, hugging the outer perimeter, making the bright green leaves of spring appear dipped in gold. Through the open car window she could inhale the crisp, clear air touched with a faint residue of winter. It was the kind of morning for special things, one of those perfect times when everything between heaven and earth is in total harmony. A sense of inner anticipation filled her.

"Wake up, we're here."

Daniel's quiet command drew Jenny's attention. She had been so engrossed in the spectacular scenery she had not realized they had parked in a small visitors' area. Off to their left was a long, low stable, flanked on each side by enclosures. In the smaller of the corrals, two saddled horses stood patiently waiting.

"Are we going to ride those?" Jenny asked doubtfully on seeing the size of the equine pair.

Even from where she sat she could see they were huge. She had ridden before, but not on animals this size. The larger, a brown and white pinto, chose that moment to throw up his head and neigh his impatience. His trail mate sidled nervously at the shrill call before adding its voice to the echoing bugle.

"I always thought trail-riding mounts were older and more placid," Jenny remarked faintly, rapidly losing the excitement and pleasure she had felt. Visions of her clinging awkwardly to the tangled mane of a runaway horse rose in her mind.

Daniel reached for her hand and gave it a reassuring squeeze. "Come on. I give you my word, you'll enjoy this."

"I'll remind you of that when the ride is over. If I remember rightly—and believe me, I do," she added with a reminiscent grimace of her last time astride, "my body is going to protest."

Daniel chuckled. "Probably, but it'll be worth it. Just wait."

Jenny had to admit Daniel's prediction was a definite understatement. Once they had crossed the sunlit meadow and entered the fringe of trees, she found herself in a long-forgotten time. It was easy to imagine she and Daniel were the only two people in the wilderness. The steady clip clop of muffled hoofbeats, the creak of leather and the faint jingle of bridles contributed to the magical effect.

Was this how the pioneer woman felt as she followed her man through the untracked mountains? Her eyes traced the lean strength of Daniel's mounted figure. Admiring the way he seemed to flow into his horse, Jenny tried to copy his easy assurance.

"How're you doing?" he questioned with a glance over his shoulder. He studied her carefully rigid figure. "Do you know why western saddles are built the way they are?"

Jenny shook her head, concentrating on not disgracing herself.

"To allow the rider to be as relaxed and as comfortable as possible while he spent the day over rough terrain."

Jenny grinned weakly at the thinly veiled reference to her stiff posture. "Is that your way of telling me to relax?"

Daniel slowed his mount as the trail widened enough for him to ride abreast. "You have a very good seat for someone who's only been up a couple of times, so why not." He leaned over and loosened her strangle grip on the saddlehorn. "Now put this hand on your thigh, and hold the reins in your right hand like I showed you," he directed, patiently.

Feeling very insecure but determined not to let him see it, Jenny did as he ordered. She was surprised at how much easier it was. Slowly she felt the tension in her body ease as she became attuned to her mare's movements. Smiling her delight, she slanted Daniel a grateful glance. "You're right. This is fun."

Arrested by the sparkling gray eyes and the laughing lips, Daniel's face softened at her uninhibited enjoyment. She had such a zest for life. Nothing like the more subdued, correct responses of the other women he had known.

For a while the two of them were silent as they wound their way through the heavily wooded, rocky terrain. Periodically, they splashed across slender ribbons of clear water, run off from the melted snows higher up. It was nearly noon when Daniel finally called a halt beside a wide creek. They were in a tiny bowl-shaped clearing bordered by trees on all sides.

Jenny slid out of the saddle, sinking ankle deep in the lush spring grass. "What a perfect place."

"I thought you'd like it." He grinned as she massaged the back of her jeans with careful hands.

"It was worth it," she agreed with an impudent chuckle while she walked about stiffly.

Daniel took the reins from her and handed her the soft cooler he had carried attached to his own saddle. "Why don't you choose where you want the picnic while I water the horses?"

Finding just the spot in a small copse of laurel, Jenny quickly spread a gay tartan blanket on the grass carpet. Overhead in the branches, a bluejay chattered at her for intruding on his solitude.

Jenny unpacked containers of crisp fried chicken

legs, potato salad, homemade blueberry muffins, big crisp pickles and assorted wedges of cheese, and, last but definitely not least, a chilled bottle of white wine. There were even two stemmed glasses to go with the colorful paper plates and plastic forks. It wasn't a picnic, it was a feast.

"Good Lord, who packs your picnics for you?" Jenny demanded as Daniel eased down beside her in front of their makeshift table.

Daniel chuckled at her amazed expression. Reaching for a small unopened plastic square, he removed the lid, revealing an array of crisp vegetables from cucumbers to broccoli tufts. "There should be a pot of dip in there, too," he said, surveying the food in front of him. His forehead puckered in a frown. "Where are the brownies? We didn't leave them in the car, did we?"

Giggling, Jenny drew out the missing brownies from under the corner of the blanket. She waved the carton triumphantly. "Fooled you."

Jenny had a split second to read the devilish retaliation to her teasing that lit Daniel's eyes before he lunged for her. Belatedly, she tried to roll away, but he caught her, pinning her to the blanket with his body. Wriggling in an attempt to dislodge him, she braced her hands against his shoulders and pushed with all her strength.

"Huh uhm," Daniel growled, trapping her flailing legs with one steel-strong calf as he rolled slightly to one side. Using his shoulder and one hand to pinion her arms, he held her captive.

Gasping for breath, Jenny glared threateningly at her captor. "Just wait until I get my hands free."

Daniel lowered his tawny head, blocking out the leafy canopy overhead. "What will you do?" he questioned in a soft, husky drawl. His lips inched closer to Jenny's.

"Push you in the creek," she murmured, breathlessly, feeling the rising desire in him. Overwhelmed by the masculine need blazing from the blue flame scorching her face, Jenny had no defense against her own feminine response. "You need a cold shower," she purred in a throaty whisper.

"Is that so?"

Daniel's mouth covered her parted lips before Jenny could form a reply. His lips moved softly, coaxingly along hers, a total contrast to the primitive way he held her prisoner. Unprepared for the gentle, seductive approach, Jenny gave in without even token resistance. What his lips asked for, his tongue took, filling her mouth with darting shivers of pleasure as he probed the deepest recesses. There was something erotically stimulating about being held totally helpless for his delicate assault, Jenny discovered. A need born of the deepest feminine desire rose within her. Arching her body against Daniel's weight, she struggled for release, freedom to bind him to her, to hold him as he was holding her.

She moaned at the continued restraint. Suddenly she no longer felt her wrists manacled by Daniel's fingers. In a blink, she wound her arms around his neck in clinging bonds of silk. "You feel so good," she breathed as her fingers dug into the smooth-muscled shoulders.

"Not nearly as good as you taste," Daniel denied, taking tiny love bites along the line of her throat to the open neck of her blouse.

Jenny felt the warmth of his breath against the valley between her breasts, then the feather-light pressure of his hand as he undid the buttons of her shirt. Opening heavy eyelids, Jenny gazed into Daniel's eyes. Losing herself in the indigo depths, she pleaded for the fulfillment she knew he could give her.

"I want you," she groaned in an aching whisper. "So much." There, she had said it. She wanted Daniel too much to deny herself. She longed to give her body completely into his keeping. This desire to belong to him had been building since that Friday night.

Tenderness replaced some of the driving need in Daniel's eyes as he took in the slightly swollen lips, the pleading eyes and tousled hair falling across her smooth brow and lightly flushed cheeks. His hand lay cradled in the hollow between her breasts, feeling the rapid heartbeat of arousal. For a second, the instinct to take what was his warred with the strange protectiveness he had for her.

Jenny saw the indecision in his expression and wondered at it. She watched the flames die in his eyes and felt the warmth of his hand leave her breast. Disappointed and unbelievably hurt by his seeming rejection, she lowered her lashes, wanting to block out the sight of his face. For the second time, she had shown him how much she wanted him and he had turned her down. Damn! Hadn't she learned anything in all her years. How often did she need to be told she was not wanted, she wondered in despair.

"Jenny, look at me." Daniel's command reached out to her across the agony she was creating for herself. "I know what you're thinking. It's not true."

Jenny heard the reassurance and the truth in his voice. Clinging to it like a candle in the darkness, she slowly opened her eyes. She saw the gentleness, tenderness, concern and something else reflected in the blue gaze. He cupped a hand under her chin, his fingers closing gently around her slender throat.

"I didn't bring you here to seduce you. If that had been my aim, I would have chosen a more comfortable place." He searched her face intently. "I wanted to spend time with you, talk to you, laugh with you.

Can you understand that? After what you said last night, I realized I couldn't possess just your body. It has to be all or nothing for us. And I need time to . . ." He hesitated, strangely at a loss for words. How did he explain what he barely understood himself? How could he tell an innocent he wanted something more than a body?

Jenny had no difficulty comprehending his meaning. "You mean until you sort out how you feel, you don't want to . . ." She waved her hand graphically at their entwined figures.

He nodded. "Surprising as it seems, I've acquired a conscience where you're concerned." He frowned darkly. "Damned inconvenient *and* uncomfortable it is, too," he muttered with thwarted masculine desire. "I've never taken so many cold showers in my life." He rolled away from Jenny's soft body in one smooth motion and lay on his back with his head cradled in his hands. "You'd better button up."

Hiding a tiny smile of feminine amusement, Jenny bent her head to do as he suggested. So. The great Daniel Masters, Knoxville's favorite bachelor, was having as much trouble as she was adjusting to this potent chemistry between them. The knowledge filled her with renewed hope for the future. While Daniel definitely didn't have the look of a man deeply in love, he certainly had proved himself not to be a seducer. He was listening to his better instincts even if they were torturing him—and they were, if his expression was anything to go by. Poor thing! she sympathized with a mental giggle. I'll bet he wouldn't be having this soul searching with one of his little blond blossoms, she thought with a funny sense of self-satisfaction. Suddenly Jenny was very hungry.

"I'm starved! May we eat now?" she demanded.

Sitting up with a smile that didn't quite reach his eyes, Daniel accepted the plate Jenny thrust at him.

"Okay, I'll take four brownies and a chicken leg," he decided in an attempt to recapture their earlier mood.

Jenny recognized the forced quality of his banter, but she ignored it. Now more than ever, she was content to wait. As she had to choose between her own philosophy and her need of this man, so too must Daniel. The mental communication they shared told her he was waging a war within himself. A war that meant the difference between a fleeting physical relationship and a deeper emotional commitment.

Lunch passed in light conversation, neither of them making any effort to confront the issue lying between them. Jenny gathered the plates and plastic forks when they were finished and packed them away for disposal later.

Daniel divided the remaining wine equally in their glasses before handing the bottle to Jenny.

"You shouldn't have given me any more. I'm liable to fall out of the saddle as it is," Jenny commented lightly as she took the glass Daniel held out.

Reclining on his side, his head propped on one hand, he lifted his wine in a gesture of salute. "There's no need to rush back. You won't have any trouble staying upright by the time we leave." He sipped the liquid gold slowly, his eyes watching her across the rim. "I was hoping we could take a little nap."

Startled by his suggestion, Jenny took a hasty gulp with the inevitable results. "Here?" she gasped when she could breathe again. "I thought you said this was one of the main trails?"

Daniel's expression showed his amusement at her reaction. "We left that a good hour before we stopped." He glanced around appreciatively. "We're far enough off the beaten path so we won't be disturbed." He swung back to study her expressive face. "Unless of course, you don't want to share the blanket with me?" His voice deepened suggestively.

Jenny didn't know what to think. A short time ago he rejected her; now he appeared bent on restoking the barely banked fires between them. "I thought you said seduction wasn't on the list of the day's activities?" she ventured after a short pause. She waited, half hoping he would take up her veiled challenge.

"What has relaxing got to do with seduction?" Daniel asked blandly, his eyes partially shielded by hooded lashes. He gently rotated the empty glass he held, seemingly intent on the way the sun sparkled off its clear surface.

"Nothing," Jenny mumbled, draining her own wine. Damn him for baiting her; he knew what he did to her.

After putting her glass in its protective wrapper in the cooler, she lay down on one edge of the blanket. She was determined not to give Daniel any more openings. If he wanted to take a nap, that was fine with her, she decided. Purposely turning her head away from the long figure stretched out only inches away, she studied the softly bubbling stream. In a matter of minutes, the soothing sound of the water and the heat of the ground beneath the blanket made her lashes flutter closed. Beside her, she could hear Daniel's deep, even breathing, indicating that he too had succumbed to the peace of their hideaway. She drifted deep into a soft cocoon of gentle rhythm and warmth.

Something warm and moist nuzzled Jenny's ear, making her raise one hand to brush at the intruder with a sleepy lack of aim. Turning her head blindly in the direction of the compelling heat stretching against her side, she sighed contentedly. A tiny nip on the lobe of her other ear reached her consciousness.

"Mm, you taste even better than you did this morning."

The sound of a very seductive, very familiar drawl brought immediate alertness to her sleep-dulled brain. Her pulse speeded up its beat as she opened her eyes and gazed into the deep indigo ones only inches away. For a moment in time, Jenny lost herself in the deep waters of slumbering desire.

Carefully, as though fearful of frightening her, Daniel gathered Jenny's body close. Still not speaking, though his eyes searched out every nuance of expression on Jenny's face, he began to kiss her, trailing light, gentle caresses over her lips, her cheekbones and across her temples. Disarmed by the leisurely exploration of her face, Jenny's lashes dropped to enclose her in a sensual darkness of awakening pleasure. Tiny flicks of Daniel's tongue brushed across her closed eyes in an unbelievably stimulating gesture. As his mouth returned to her lips, his hands began a slow glide down her spine to her hips, pulling her more firmly against him until Jenny was aware of the hardening masculine desire.

"Daniel!" Jenny gasped in excited anticipation. Her smoky gray eyes drifted open to fasten on Daniel's lean face. The warmth and tenderness she saw echoed her own emotions.

She felt his hands tug her shirt from her waistband and then slide beneath it to seek the smooth, ivory skin. The top was in the way, Jenny thought hazily, her own hands busy with the buttons on Daniel's shirt. She wanted the feel of him against her bare skin. As her fingers pushed the soft cotton off his shoulders, she felt a light draft of air across her breasts.

"God, you're beautiful," Daniel murmured, his eyes drinking in the sight of her pale perfection. He made a sound deep in the back of his throat, and his hands came up to gently cradle the soft rose-tipped peaks. At his touch, they seemed to swell in glorious pride to fill his waiting palms. His fingers had a life of their own as they stroked and kneaded the lush curves, while his mouth tasted its way from her lips down the arch of her throat to the rich treasures he held.

Jenny burned with the sensations Daniel created. Her own hands explored the tawny pelt covering his chest. His body gave off heat like a bonfire, burning her searching fingers whenever they touched the skin beneath golden fur.

A ripple of exquisite pain radiated through her as Daniel fastened on one nipple. She felt his tongue roll over the crest as it blossomed under his caress. She moaned as he suckled gently like a babe. She writhed in increasing desire, her hips arching into the body beside her.

"Delicious," Daniel murmured into the valley between her breasts. He lifted his head, gazing deep into the swirling mists of passion of Jenny's eyes. "I want you, every beautiful inch of you," he whispered in an urgent demand for surrender. "Come to me."

Unable to deny him, Jenny pulled his head down to meet her avid mouth, giving him the answer he sought by the hungry assault of her lips. How she wanted him, needed what only he could give.

Gently removing her jeans in a motion so smooth Jenny was hardly aware of it, he exposed the exquisite length of her to his blazing eyes. The kisses he had bestowed before were only an appetizer for what followed. Now that he had the freedom of her body, he seemed intent on claiming every inch of the silky skin. His mouth was a fiery brand as he sipped and feasted on his possession. Moaning with desire, aching with need, Jenny's hands sought to claim her own reward. Divesting him of his jeans, she stroked and kneaded the tanned muscles beneath her finger-tips. Encouraged by the ever-deepening rasp of Daniel's breath, the animal growl of desire against her abdomen, she arched violently against him in mute demand for his invasion. There was a mo-ment's hesitation as Daniel prepared himself, then, answering her appeal, Daniel spread her thighs gently to take what was his alone. Jenny clung to him, reveling in his tenderness and his desire for her. Her hands splayed over the bunched muscles of his back, digging for a purchase as he lifted her to complete their union. His first thrust entered the virgin territory forever branding it as his.

Jenny muffled her cry against the smooth, glisten-ing swell of his shoulder. Kissing his neck, his throat, anything she could reach, she went wild beneath his rhythmic stroking. Deeper and deeper he plunged into the rich cave of womanhood until the whole world dissolved into a cloudy mist of sensation-burning desire bursting through the dam of restraint.

"Daniel." It was an echoing cry of fulfillment torn from the very core of her femininity.

"Jenny!" A masculine exaltation of the conqueror.

Jenny lost herself in Daniel, unable to tell or care where her body ended and his began. Here was no meadow, no trees, or horses, only the oneness of their consumation.

For a long time neither of them stirred, content to lie replete, satisfied in their mutual embrace. Finally, Daniel raised his head from Jenny's shoulder. His eyes carried a depth of feeling Jenny had never seen before.

It was love! Jenny knew it as surely as she knew the sweet intoxication of his body.

"This isn't at all as I planned it," Daniel murmured. His finger traced lightly down Jenny's throat to her breasts. "I planned to go slowly so we could get to know each other." He smiled crookedly at his own inability to stick to his plan. "Marry me, Jenny. I can't wait for all the right moves to happen. Come and be my wife, my love."

The demanding plea was lost against Jenny's lips as she reached eagerly for her lover, the man of her dreams.

8

⚬⚬⚬⚬⚬⚬⚬⚬⚬⚬

You're what?" Maggie demanded in stunned accents.

"I'm going to get married," Jenny repeated, patiently, a small smile playing at her lips as she viewed Maggie's incredulous expression.

Her friend sank limply into her chair, eyeing Jenny's relaxed figure as she leaned casually against her work table. "To who?" Although gramatically incorrect, her question was further evidence of her total surprise.

"Daniel Masters."

"The Daniel Masters?" Maggie echoed in a shriek. "I didn't even know you were dating! Now you meet me at the door with something like this!" She studied Jenny suspiciously. "You're just teasing me, aren't you?"

Jenny shook her head, laughter bubbling light-heartedly to the surface. Maggie's feelings were almost a mirror image of her own. It was hard to believe Daniel had proposed. She stopped. Although, come to think of it, he hadn't. He had told her they were getting married. A reminiscent smile touched her face, the memory of the sunlit meadow darkening her eyes.

"My Gawd," Maggie's southern drawl had never been more pronounced. "When I said you needed a Prince Charming, I didn't mean that literally." Her plump face reflected her concern. "How on earth did you meet him? How long have you two been seeing each other?"

Recognizing Maggie's worry, Jenny straightened and went over to take the chair opposite the older woman. The laughter died. This was her life they were talking about. She didn't need Maggie's blessing, but she valued her down-to-earth opinions. She wanted her approval though she knew she would marry Daniel with or without it.

"Maggie, be happy for me, please," she pleaded. "I know we haven't known each other long, and I know how different our lives are. But I love him. He loves me." She extended her hand, palm up, across the table. "Please, Maggie, if I have any family, it's you." Smoke-gray eyes begged for understanding.

Maggie's kind face crumpled before the strength of Jenny's determination. Tears welled in her aged eyes. "Oh, honey, you know I want you to be happy." She clasped the slender fingers with loving force. She smiled through her tears. "If he's the one you want, that's all there is to say."

Returning the pressure of Maggie's hold, Jenny mirrored her smile. "I knew I could count on you," she teased in an effort to lighten the atmosphere. "I'm going to need your expertise to get me outfitted for my role." Sudden doubts assailed her as she realized she didn't possess an outfit in her entire wardrobe that was suitable for the wife of one of the wealthiest men in Knoxville. At least she had a few fairly nice things, thanks to Maggie's bullying.

Unaware of Jenny's anxiety, Maggie got caught up in the romance of their plans. "When are ya'll goin' for the engagement ring?"

"At noon." Her startled shriek of dismay followed quickly on the heels of her answer. "It's time to open and I haven't done a thing so far this morning!" She grabbed her oversized handbag from the drawer in her work table and thrust the bank pouch in Maggie's direction. Picking up the bag, Maggie rose and headed for the main shop area.

Jenny eyed her retreating figure, a reluctant smile tugging at the frown on her lips. Easing her smock on, she went to her order board. Daniel or no, she still had a business to run. And that meant getting on with it. At the rate she was going, she wouldn't be ready by closing time, much less lunch. For a fleeting second, she wondered what would happen to Eden when she married. For the life of her, she couldn't imagine Edna Masters wanting a florist daughter-in-law.

A cloud of doubt darkened the sunny future. Lost in a world of Daniel's love, she had forgotten for a moment the world she would be entering. Edna Masters was sure to disapprove, no matter how distantly pleasant she had been in the past. No! She wouldn't think of her background. Daniel had said he loved her and admired and respected her accomplishments. She would not let anyone else's opinion matter.

Whether it was the usual hectic Monday morning schedule after the Dogwood Ball or the fact that Jenny's concentration seemed to have deserted her, she had just barely finished when she heard Daniel's slow, distinct voice in the display room.

Slipping quickly out of her work smock, she hardly had a chance to brush her fingers through her tousled hair in a vain attempt to restore some order to the layered curls. She wished she had had time to go upstairs and put on a fresh shirt and maybe retouch her careful makeup. She turned to greet Daniel and found him standing just inside the doorway between the main shop and the workroom. There was no sign of Maggie, Jenny realized vaguely as she stared silently into Daniel's face. In the back of her mind even as she raced to complete the day's orders, she had wondered how Daniel would act when she saw him. Never having had a lover, much less a fiancé before, she had no idea what to expect. Now she knew!

Without a word or a touch, Daniel made her his again. The sunlight of their mountain hideaway warmed her skin in the wake of the indigo sweep of his eyes. They caressed her from the top of her head to the tip of her toes and back to her lips, curling around her, immeshing her in a web of remembered passion. Jenny's eyes darkened to smoke as he strolled lazily toward her, never taking his gaze from her mouth. His breath fanned her face when he bent his head to capture the soft fullness already parting for his possession. His hands settled on her shoulders, drawing her into the strength of him until Jenny melted against his muscled flesh in an effort to become one again. Her eyes drifted shut, the better to savor the feel and scent of her man.

Passionate, demanding, hot with undisguised male need, his kiss drew an equally hungry response from Jenny. Yesterday, he had introduced her to the pleasures and desires of love. Today, she ached for another lesson. Oblivious of possible interruption, she wound her arms around his neck, seeking to bind him to her forever. A low groan echoed in the silence. Was it hers? His? Or both of them? The tiny sound broke the spell.

Slowly, reluctantly Daniel lowered the fire raging between them. His devouring tongue gently soothed Jenny's tender mouth and finally the soft inner line of her lips. As he withdrew completely, he teased the bottom curve with a tiny nip that brought Jenny's lashes open with startled surprise.

"Have you been thinking about me as much as I've been thinking about you?" he questioned whimsically. His sensitive fingers waltzed down Jenny's spine to tug her firmly against his hips.

Feeling the hardness against her tender curves, Jenny shook her head, hiding the teasing glint in her eyes by leaning her forehead on his chest. "Not quite as much as you have, but then I haven't had as much practice, either."

She knew she should be feeling shy with Daniel, or at least slightly restrained. After all, it had been the first time for her. Yet she didn't feel any such inhibitions; in fact, quite the opposite. She wanted him, and she saw no reason to hide the fact. It never had been her way in the past, and it wouldn't be her way in the future.

Daniel rallied swiftly in the brief pause. He gave her a small admonishing shake before releasing her completely. "The day you stop surprising me . . ." he began, his eyes lighting with humorous understanding. He took her arm and guided her toward the front door without completing his thought. "Let's go, before I spend the rest of the afternoon giving you what you deserve."

"A hiding?" Jenny drawled sweetly, casting him an impish glance.

"No, ma'am. I'm not so uncivilized," Daniel denied solemnly, ushering her out onto the sidewalk. With a brief farewell wave at Maggie, Jenny meekly followed the pressure of Daniel's grip.

* * *

When they arrived at the small jewelry shop, Jenny looked around her with interest. She had heard of Zodiac Gems—who in Knoxville hadn't. It was *the* place to go for the unusual, the rare and the distinctive. The owner was a master craftsman who excelled in one-of-a-kind designs.

The gnomelike little owner, recognizing Knoxville's most influential citizen, personally greeted Daniel and Jenny at the door. Ushering them to a secluded viewing alcove, he waited until they were comfortably seated before presenting a royal blue velvet display tray of rings for their inspection. The glittering array displayed stones in a myriad of rich colors. There was gold and silver with rubies, sapphires, emeralds, amethysts and diamonds.

Jenny's mind boggled at making a selection. She raised her eyes to Daniel's in helpless appeal. For a moment, she felt the touch of his mind as he read the confusion and indecision in hers. His fingers tightened on her hand, reassuring her.

He turned to the owner with a courteous smile. "It may take us a minute," he explained in a polite hint for the man to leave them alone to make their choice.

It was a measure of the Masters' influence that the proprietor quickly granted his request.

"You choose," Jenny pleaded in a low voice.

Daniel shook his head, the warmth in his eyes reflecting gentle understanding. "No, we both will." He picked up a glowing green marquise emerald set in gold and surrounded by diamonds. "How about this one?"

The size of the ring alone made Jenny catch her breath. "It's huge," she protested, mentally picturing herself losing the expensive ring in one of her flower arrangements when she was working. Again it occurred to her that her days as a manual helper in her shop were numbered.

A frown touched Daniel's face at her comment while he returned the circle to the tray and picked out another slightly smaller cluster, this one of diamonds. Each time Jenny demurred until Daniel finally pushed the tray to one side.

Turning her to face him in the swivel chair, he placed one hand on each arm rest effectively trapping her in her seat. "What in the devil has gotten into you, Jenny?" he demanded in rising frustration.

Jenny glanced evasively around in the tiny private viewing alcove, anywhere except into Daniel's shrewd probing eyes. How could she explain her feelings when she didn't understand them herself? She knew she wanted to be Daniel's wife. Unconsciously, he had been the man she had measured all others by. Yet, now that her fantasy had become a reality, she was assailed by doubts. Was she good enough for him? How easily he sat in front of thousands of dollars in precious stones, casually asking her to select her favorite. For the first time, the tangible reality of having practically unending wealth swept over her. She felt ill-equipped to deal with the life he led. Any other woman would give her eye-teeth to be in her shoes, she admitted with a burst of self-analysis. The old orphan Jenny—the part of her she had thought she had buried—was filling her with doubts.

"Jenny, talk to me." Daniel's command was softened with a note of pleading.

It was that vulnerability that Jenny responded to. "Daniel, don't you see: I'm not right for you," she blurted in a rush. She waved her hand at the tray of jewels. "I'm afraid of all of this. What will happen when we marry? I don't know a diamond from a piece of quartz. The only reason I know the difference between a ruby and an emerald is one's red and the other's green.

"Who gives a damn, Jenny!" Daniel exploded. "I sure don't. I couldn't care less what you don't know. It's you and what you are that I love. Do you think I know everything? I can't even convince the woman I'm going to marry that I love her." He leaned forward, determination in every line of his lean body. His face was bone taut with the force of his anger and his need to dispel her fears. "I *know* you're an orphan. I *know* you have the damnedest insecurity complex. But you're a fighter, a survivor. You've got courage to face the seemingly insurmountable and win." He lifted his hands to frame her face. "You're afraid to share my life. It should be the easiest thing in the world for you to come to me. And it isn't. I know, because I *see* it and I *feel* it."

Tears lent a shimmer of liquid silver to Jenny's eyes. "I love you, Daniel. Believe that, please. It's just that it's so hard to accept the changes that I see coming. I'm terrified of failing you—and myself. Before it's only been me to worry about."

Daniel's thumbs stroked gently across her chin, then moved upward to her lips as she finished speaking. Gazing into her anxious face, he recognized the plea for understanding. He gave it. "Don't you think I know that?" He bent his head to brush her lips with a light kiss. "Now I have a plan—one that should get rid of some of these plaguing irritants that are cluttering up our engagement." This last was said on such a teasing note of whimsy Jenny's attention was immediately caught.

She stared at him, curiosity replacing some of her doubts.

"You and I are going to take this one day at a time. You aren't the only one with worries, you know."

Jenny's eyes widened at that. What did he mean?

"Just look at me. I'm pushing forty and I haven't the slightest idea about how to be a husband. Not only that, I have a positive mania about forgetting birthdays, anniversaries, et cetera. And *I know* a husband is supposed to be a paragon of memory," he countered in an attempt to draw a smile from Jenny. "That's the main reason we're getting the biggest ring I can convince you to accept. I figure if it's large enough, I'll be able to remember one date, anyway."

The absurdity of Daniel, a man known throughout the state for his business acumen, needing so blatant a reminder, struck Jenny as funny—as she suspected he knew it would. "You win," she surrendered on a chuckle. "We'll get the biggest stone this shop has. As a dutiful wife, I can't let an opportunity to be helpful to my husband slip through my fingers."

Jenny's words were joking, but there was no amusement in the loving gratitude of her eyes. Once again Daniel had exhibited his ability to sense her thoughts and to respond to her deepest needs. Her doubts still remained, but not nearly as frightening as they had been.

"I knew I could count on you."

For a second their eyes locked in a single direct flow of mental communication. Jenny felt the warmth of his love, the reassurance of his faith in her. In return, she gave him her trust, her heart. As one, they turned to resume their search for an engagement ring.

"What about that one?" Daniel asked a few minutes later, after signaling for the owner to assist them. He indicated a small purple velvet box sitting open on the top display shelf of the glass counter.

Jenny's eyes fastened on the delicate creation with delight. It was exquisitely beautiful, a tiny, intricately perfect silver flower. Each petal was a pale lavender amethyst, and the center was a small cut gem of a slightly deeper shade. Raised off the gleaming silver band like a blossom on a short stem, it was flanked on each side by a lifelike emerald-jeweled leaf.

"It's not really an engagement ring, as you can see, Mr. Masters," the owner explained as he withdrew the box from its resting place.

"It's beautiful," Jenny murmured in awe.

Daniel lifted the flower ring from its bed of velvet. Taking Jenny's left hand, he slipped it gently on her finger. It fit as though it had been made especially for her.

Bemused by the delicate shimmer of the stones, Jenny moved her hand slowly from side to side before raising her eyes to Daniel.

"Do you like it?" he asked unnecessarily. He was able to read her answer in her glowing face. She nodded shyly, causing him to exchange a satisfied smile with the man who had designed the ring.

"We'll take it."

Jenny was entranced with her gift. Loving flowers the way she did made the ring even more special to her.

"You were wearing that shade of lavender the first time we met. Do you remember?" Daniel asked softly when they got in the car.

Surprised at his recall, Jenny could only nod.

"Of course the flowers you held weren't nearly as beautiful as this one," he went on, watching her reaction closely.

Memory of the weed-filled chamber pot colored Jenny's cheeks with embarrassment. "Are you going to remind me of that every chance you get?" she demanded, half seriously. Of all the moments they shared, this was the one she most desired to forget.

"Probably," Daniel admitted in answer to her

question. "I think I fell a little in love with you that day."

Jenny's expression reflected her skepticism. "I don't see how," she murmured in honest puzzlement.

Daniel lightly brushed the side of her neck in a beguiling caress, his blue eyes warm and steady on hers. "Maybe because I felt the regret in you for your part in Lilly's dramatics. Or could it have been the brave way you stood there facing me after Penny fled? You looked so damned scared and determined not to show it." His fingers traced the contours of the top of her shirt lingering on the pulsating hollow of her throat.

Drawn by the awareness Daniel was creating, Jenny raised her face to his. It made no difference that it was broad daylight in the middle of a busy street. She felt the desire building within, demanding release. Daniel was like a drug in her system—an addiction she welcomed gladly. Her eyes filled with the smoke of rapidly mounting passion.

"Damn this afternoon's appointments," Daniel muttered hoarsely moving the last inches to capture her lips.

Jenny echoed his words in her mind as she accepted the invading warmth of his mouth. Eager lips parted, giving and seeking the secrets of their hidden pleasures. She drank of him, once again reaching for the essence that was Daniel. The hand carrying his pledge circled his neck, the amethyst flower glimmering seductively in the golden strands of hair at the nape. Her other hand found its way to the buttons of his shirt, burrowing into the opening her agile fingers created. She arched against Daniel's hand as he sought the heavy fullness of her rich breast.

"My love," Daniel said huskily against her ear,

trapping her questing fingers with the weight of his body, "you drive me past the point of sanity."

Bereft of his lips, Jenny nibbled at the tanned column of his neck, working her way up to his jaw. He tasted so good. The clean scent of him filled her senses, driving her wild with need. She moaned in protest as the raging blaze was slowly brought under control.

"Hush, Jenny, easy," Daniel soothed, his hands moving to quiet the tempest he had spawned. He held her trembling body until Jenny lay still against him, her head nestled under his chin.

"I thought it would be safe to kiss you here. I can see I was wrong," he drawled wryly, his voice betraying his own state of arousal. "I don't know what it is about you, but every time I'm around your delectable little shape, I go up in flames." He eased Jenny's pliant body back against the seat, dropping a brief, hard kiss on her lips as he did so. "I hope you're planning on the shortest engagement and the fastest marriage in history."

Jenny flicked him a slightly teasing look. She was amazed at her own passion and the ease with which her body responded. She knew no feeling of regret or shame. Their love was a natural extension of their deep communication, their merging of spirits. "The sooner the better," she agreed with feeling. "Much more of this and I won't see my next birthday."

Daniel's full-throated chuckle showed his appreciation of her sally. "You're a woman in a million," he stated in sincere admiration. He started the car.

"Why? Because I agree with you?"

"No, because you're honest enough to admit how you feel. It's a rare commodity in this world." The sudden hardening cynicism in his voice drew an instant protest.

"Don't, Daniel."

He glanced at her, hearing the touch of fear in her tone with surprise. "Don't what?"

"Don't put me on a pedestal. I couldn't bear it. I want to be a woman, your woman. I couldn't survive my failure to live up to the image you created." She stared at him, willing him to understand how very important he had become to her existence. How could she really explain how much she was coming to depend on the security of his love and reassurance. He was a haven, a family, a lover and a friend. Where he was, home was.

"You won't fail me, Jenny. Not now, not ever." Daniel's voice reached out to give her the words she needed. "I chose you . . . we chose each other knowing the best and the worst." He flashed a teasing look. "I know you've got a few bad habits."

"Name one."

"The way you worry about your lack of background," he ventured, suddenly serious. "*That* I'm going to change."

Jenny was surprised at the raw determination in his tone. "How?" she questioned curiously, seeing her shop come into view.

"By filling your life with everything you think you've missed. When I was growing up, I always wanted someone to spoil rotten, and now I've got my wish."

He parked the Porsche expertly in the narrow street, stopping a few feet from her door. Switching off the engine, he turned to her, a devilish glint in his eye that Jenny didn't trust one inch. "Yesterday was just the beginning."

Intrigued by his air of leashed anticipation, Jenny felt like a child waiting for Christmas morning. Well, not quite like a child, she admitted catching the smouldering flame of desire in Daniel's blue gaze. He leaned across her, his hand deliberately caressing her taut breasts and opened the door. Jenny sucked in her breath in an audible gasp, drawing a twisted grin. "Hell, isn't it?" Daniel grinned.

"It's not the most comfortable I've ever been," Jenny shot back pertly, exiting the car speedily to escape Daniel's retribution.

"Be ready at seven," Daniel called after her retreating figure. "Wear something sexy." He laughed out loud at the expression of outrage he saw as she glared over her shoulder at him.

Honest and uninhibited with him, she still was a reserved, private person in public. The thought pleased him enormously. He had never cared what his women were before he knew them. But Jenny was different. Innocent, wise, tantalizing, provocative —a modern woman with a touch of old-world values. The contrast was stimulating, it was an exhilarating challenge to his manhood to arouse the sensual woman he knew existed beneath the mask she wore in public.

Jenny had no idea of Daniel's thoughts that evening as she soaked in a warm tub. She had enough of her own. Sexy! She smiled complacently at the word. So he wants sexy, does he? She slowly lathered her arms and then across her shoulders to her throat. Mentally, she pictured the orchid dress she had played hooky from her afternoon schedule to find. Unconsciously, her bath sponge moved caressingly over her breasts in a reminiscent motion of Daniel's hands. Heat stirred in her at his certain reaction.

It was deceptively simple—little more than an Oriental tunic of fine raw silk. It was the perfect gown to complement her ring. But the part Daniel was sure to appreciate was the thigh-high slash that showcased her legs. And that wasn't all. The neckline was no modest plunge, either. A brassiere was definitely out.

"I hope your blood pressure's up to it, Daniel, my love," she giggled with a very feminine instinct to get to her man. Tease her in the middle of the street in front of half of Knoxville and God only knows who else, would he? She'd show him not to rattle her cage.

Daniel's arrival at her apartment coincided exactly with the last touch to Jenny's image. She strolled unhurriedly to the door, trailing an elusive scent of Arabesque.

He stood waiting for her with a small pale green box in one hand, his eyes sweeping possessively over her.

"Flowers?" she queried with surprise, recognizing her own florist colors.

He extended his gift with a nod, his other hand snaking out to encircle her waist in one smooth motion as he stepped inside, closing the door behind him.

"Dan—" Jenny's startled protest was swallowed in mid-word by his hungry lips.

When his mouth covered hers, Jenny responded eagerly to his desire. Every time he touched her, this need to burn in the flames of passion grew stronger.

"Aren't you going to open your present?" he murmured against her lips.

Swirls of smoky mist dueled with twin blue fires as Jenny debated whether to laugh or not speak. Darn him for greeting her that way. The last thing on her mind now was flowers.

"You know you're not *really* angry," he coaxed, fully aware of the havoc he was causing. He trailed a lazy finger down the narrow slit opening between her breasts and explored the contours of the satiny mounds.

"I can't very well be with you holding me," Jenny gasped as the room spun.

Scooping her against his chest, he strode over to the sofa and sat down with her in his lap.

Jenny was held prisoner by the curve of the massive couch and Daniel's arms. As she struggled halfheartedly for her freedom, the slit in her skirt rode higher, exposing the full sleek length of her legs.

"Don't you dare," she panted breathlessly as she felt his warm hand slide sensuously up her thigh and across her hips. "I didn't get all dressed up for you to make me look like I've been romping in the hay. Daniel Masters!" The last came out on a wail of undeniable desire. The package tumbled unheeded to the floor as Jenny gave herself up to the exquisite delight of his caress. She felt his fingers at the tiny buttons at the base of the neck opening.

"You know you like it." Daniel's husky whisper fanned along her exposed breasts. His mouth captured one rosy peak, his tongue curling warmly around the swollen bud.

"Yes, Daniel," she moaned, her head falling back against his shoulder as she arched her body to meet his mouth.

She was scarcely aware of her fingers digging into his shoulders as his other hand tugged the tiny wisp of lace panties down over her hips. The teasing fingers that delved into the silky brown curls blazed a trail fire to the very core of her femininity.

"You feel so good, so warm and moist." The erotic massage went on just tantalizingly out of reach.

"Daniel!" It was a demanding plea for the release of the passionate flood building within.

Mindlessly caught up in the raging torrent of need,

Jenny pulled his head up to meet her lips. She wanted him in her, with her, holding her. Jacket and shirt seemed to melt away under her eager hands. She whimpered in pure animal pleasure when her dress followed his clothes to the floor. Pressing her naked curves against the lean muscled frame, she reveled in the rough rasp of his pelt across her tender breasts.

"God, woman," Daniel murmured against her ear. His hand roamed up her abdomen to her breasts. "What about dinner?" he questioned, raising his head for a second to gaze into her eyes.

"Later," Jenny purred with point-blank honesty. "You've got too many clothes on."

What little control Daniel still retained evaporated under Jenny's passionate response. In a matter of seconds, Daniel had slipped out of his shoes and trousers and lifted her once again into his arms. He held her with fierce passion as he entered her bedroom, his eyes blazing with a desire equal to hers. Wordlessly he pulled back the covers and laid her gently in the middle of the bed, following her descent with his body. He ran his hands caressingly down her spine, sinking his fingers into the curve of her bottom. He pulled her against him, letting Jenny feel the hardening of his need.

Jenny spread her fingers across his chest, exploring the rough curling fur even as his leg moved boldly between hers. She closed her eyes to savor the sensual world of his touch.

Daniel's hands gripped her hips, holding her still for their mating. At the first thrust, Jenny arched upward, a soft sighing moan escaping her lips at the swollen manhood filling her. Daniel set the rhythm of their desire. It was explosive, primitive—the most basic life-giving force known to man. Jenny responded at every turn meeting his need, his passion with an ardor so intense it seared the skin, melding the two of them into one being, a total possession of the other.

Their names cried out in exquisite pleasure of their union. Together they rode the crest until exhausted, satiated, they drifted languidly back to reality.

"You were right about dinner; I wasn't very hungry either," Daniel whispered intimately when his breathing eased somewhat. Molding Jenny's body more firmly against his own, he pulled the sheet up to cover them. "I'll let you fix me breakfast in the morning."

Jenny snuggled closer to the warmth of him, perfectly content to share her bed with him. She was drowsy, replete and totally loved.

"I hope you like Cheerios," she mumbled sleepily. The husky rumble of tender laughter close to her ear made her lips curve into a smile as she drifted off.

9

~000000000000~

Strong arms encircled Jenny from behind while she leaned over the dining table. "Better?" Daniel asked huskily, rubbing his clean-shaven jaw along the side of her cheek.

Setting down the heaping plates of bacon, eggs and grits on the gingham placemats, Jenny turned in his embrace. "Much," she agreed with a loving smile. She cradled his face between her hands, "I knew that that free sample of shaving cream would come in handy some day." She stood on tiptoe to brush her lips across his mouth.

His arms tightened around her waist, drawing her against him possessively, molding her contours to his. "Have I told you I love you yet this morning?" Daniel questioned in a deeply male voice, his gaze roaming hungrily over her glowing, sleepy-eyed face.

Jenny giggled. "Once in the shower, and at least twice every time we—" Her answer was cut off by Daniel's mouth as he captured her lips.

Jenny melted against him, eagerly meeting the demand of his probing tongue. Last night had been a revelation in the depth of their need for each other.

164

Again and again they came together in the darkness. Sometimes gentle, sometimes passionate, but always loving and deeply fulfilling.

"Breakfast is getting cold," Jenny whispered.

"Do you care?" Daniel replied, reluctantly setting her free.

Jenny tipped her head to one side, pretending to consider. "Yes," she decided, a wicked gleam in her smoky eyes. "I need my energy after that shower this morning." She took a chair, flashing him her best curious look. "Where did you learn how to . . . ah . . . play around like that?" She grinned openly at the faint tinge of red creeping under Daniel's tan.

"Jenny Brown!" It was the warning of a severely goaded male. "If you don't shut up and eat, I'll show you what else I know." He stabbed his scrambled eggs to emphasize his threat.

"I'm eating." Looking anything but frightened, Jenny picked up her own fork.

Talk was suspended while they both satisfied their hunger. Finally, Daniel leaned back with a sigh, his second cup of coffee held in one hand. "I can see I'm not going to be happy with Etta's cooking any longer," he complimented her.

Etta was the Masters' cook. Jenny had met the tiny kitchen queen during one of her catering assignments. Just the mention of her brought to mind the east Tennessee showplace of Masters heritage, Azalea Hill. Jenny felt the old sense of inadequacy return at the thought of being the mistress of the huge two-storied mansion on the knoll overlooking the river.

"By the way, my mother would like to have you out to the Hill for lunch today. She wants to show you around and get to know you better. I meant to tell you last night, but other things got in the way."

As he spoke, Daniel studied Jenny's reaction

closely. He had a good idea how anxious she was going to be. It frustrated him that she had so little confidence in her own worth. As much as he loved her, he knew it would be easier for her if she did become more secure before they were married. Realistically, he knew there were bound to be some people cruel enough to use her background against her if they could. As much as he'd like to, he couldn't always be at her side.

Jenny's doubts increased at hearing Daniel's words. She stared at him in dismay. "Meet me for lunch?" she echoed. "Are you coming, too?" She knew she would need the reassurance of his presence. She and Mrs. Masters had always gotten along well whenever they had worked together, but there was a world of difference between being a hired florist and a future daughter-in-law. The thought of facing the formidable Masters matriarch over a polite little luncheon frankly terrified her.

Daniel placed his cup carefully on the table. "Jenny, my mother won't pounce on you, I promise," he stated, leaning forward, his eyes pinning hers. "Do you think I'd send you there alone if I thought she would? She knows all about you, and she's satisfied with my choice. So try believing in yourself and trust me. By now you should be able at least to have faith in our relationship. Didn't last night tell you anything?"

"Sex isn't an answer to this, Daniel," Jenny retorted quickly and unwisely. She saw his eyes narrow, but she hurried on. "I can't help the way I am or what I'm feeling right now. My whole life is changing. I'm not just marrying you," she extended her hands palm up in a gesture of helpless defeat. "I'm entering a life-style I know nothing about. I'll live in a house as big as a hotel. Even my shop is going."

Daniel's head snapped up alertly. "What's this about the store?"

"I'll be giving it up, won't I?" Jenny answered in confusion.

"I've never asked you to do that. If I thought about it at all, I assumed you'd hire someone to replace you on a part-time basis."

Jenny's eyes reflected her pleased surprise. Forgetting for a moment the question of the impending lunch, she leaned forward eagerly. "You mean I can keep it? I can work there?" she clarified, scarcely able to believe he was telling the truth. She'd been so sure he would demand she give it up, she hadn't been able to face the possibility.

Daniel nodded, his face curiously grim. "What kind of a man do you think I am, Jennifer? I can't understand how you thought I would force you to give up ten years of work just because we're marrying. Sure, I want you home; sure, I want you free to go where I go. But I'm damned well not intending to chain you to a bed in the process."

Jenny's face reddened at his blunt words. She felt the hurt she had dealt him as her own. How could she have been so stupid? Why hadn't she just asked him about the store instead of jumping to all the wrong conclusions? She swallowed, knowing he deserved an apology.

Accurately reading her intentions, Daniel waved his hand dismissively. "Don't bother. I understand why you thought what you did, but it doesn't make it any easier to accept for either of us." He stared at her a moment in silence. "I love you, Jenny, and I know you love me. That should be the beginning and the end for us. But it isn't. You act like you can't believe in our future and me. It's time for you to let go of the past. If you don't, neither of us is going to be happy. I can't and I won't apologize for my life. It's my

167

heritage and my responsibility. If you accept my love, you must accept that part of me as well. Just as I have accepted you and your past." His voice was calm as he finished, but his words clearly portrayed the depth of his emotions. He had made his feelings known, now it was up to Jenny.

What could she say? Jenny wondered, knowing he spoke the truth. He was offering her everything of himself, his love, his life, his understanding and his problems. It was only fair to give him her total self. Not some frightened orphan, but a mature, rational thinking adult woman. She opened her mouth to tell him her decision, but Daniel gave her no chance.

"Don't say anything now, Jenny," his voice softened slightly. "Just work on it. I don't expect overnight changes but I do expect you to try."

"I'll do better, I promise," Jenny vowed from the depth of her soul.

He smiled. It was a healing balm to Jenny's regret and feelings of failing him. "How does two Saturdays from now strike you as a wedding day?" he queried on an altered note. "I wish it could be sooner, but I have an important deal in the offing. If I work like the devil between now and then, I'll be able to take at least three full weeks for our honeymoon."

"A week from Saturday?" Jenny repeated, beginning to feel like a nodding parrot. She took a firm grip on her dwindling courage. As much as she wanted to be Daniel's wife, she didn't like this rushed feeling. There was too much happening too soon. She had thought just loving Daniel and having him love her was enough. She now knew that was only part of the problem. She had to find herself, get in touch with the part of her that had never matured. She desperately needed time to come to terms with what was happening. When she had told him she had hoped for a quick marriage, she had envisioned a month or six weeks—not less than two! She saw his look of expectancy and knew she couldn't voice yet another doubt. Hadn't he just shown her how important she was to him?

"It sounds perfect," she responded injecting enthusiasm into her tone. "I'll need a dress, though. Maybe Maggie could help me."

"Or my mother," he suggested, bringing the conversation back to its starting place. "You could ask her when you see her today."

Feeling like a fraud, Jenny agreed. The last thing she wanted was Edna Masters choosing her clothes.

"There's a small chapel near the Hill. I thought it would be a perfect place for the ceremony. Unless, of course, you want a big affair?" The last was tacked on with such a blatantly hopeful appeal not to demand a spectacle that Jenny had to laugh.

"Considering how little time there is, I think a small gathering is the best idea. And I love the place you chose. It has always been my favorite church. It's so quiet and beautiful."

Daniel appeared pleased all out of proportion, Jenny thought. She knew he realized how a big fanfare would make her uncomfortable. She loved him all the more for choosing this way to let her know he didn't expect her to suffer for the sake of a social wedding.

"Now there's just one other thing."

"Only one?" Jenny returned, beginning to recapture some of her earlier lighthearted mood.

"The party this Saturday where I get to show you off."

This was a test. Jenny could see Daniel watching her every expression. She would not fail him this time.

"Good. I'd like to meet your friends." Lukewarm,

but, Jenny decided, at least her voice sounded normal.

Daniel's smile of approval rewarded her efforts. "See, that wasn't so bad." He rose to his feet and reached for her hand to pull her up beside him.

"It's not Saturday yet," Jenny muttered, leaning her head on his chest. Putting her arms around Daniel's waist, she pressed close against him. His arms wrapped around her, pulling her nearer still. One hand settled at the vulnerable base of her neck and began a slow, soothing massage of the sensitive area.

Jenny sighed in bliss, letting her lashes drift shut. When Daniel held her like this, she could believe in anything or anyone. Even herself. He was the security she needed, the love she'd never had.

"Come on, my soon-to-be wife, you'd better walk me to the door," he commanded, releasing her, yet keeping her chained to his side with an arm around her waist. "If I didn't have so damned much to do at the office, I don't think you would see the light of day until tomorrow."

Jenny chuckled at the sorely tried tone. "Just think what your mother would say if I didn't show up at Azalea Hill," Jenny teased, surprising herself by speaking of her future mother-in-law. She was tense already with just the mention of her name, but for Daniel she was determined to fight it.

"I knew there was a reason why I love you," Daniel murmured, halting at the door and turning her to face him. He bent his head, capturing her lips in a kiss that held all of the remembered pleasure of their lovemaking and all the longing he felt to stay. His hand slid in the deep V neckline of her pullover to caress one bare breast.

Jenny arched against him, achingly aware of the desire flaming to life at his touch. Heated whimpers of passion purred in her throat to be devoured by his mouth. Her hands moved around his neck to his shoulders and she kneaded like a cat, clawing in a massage that brought a groan of desire to Daniel's lips.

Tearing his mouth from hers, he pressed Jenny's head against his shoulder. "No more, I can't handle it."

Jenny heard the accelerated thud of his heart beneath her cheek with feminine satisfaction. It was so good to know her attraction for him was as powerful as his for her.

Daniel set her gently away from him. "I've got to go. I'm going to be making an overnight to Atlanta this noon, so I won't see you tonight. But I'll call you. Okay?" At her bemused nod he dropped a quick, hard kiss on her love-softened mouth before opening the door. He paused for a split second. "I'm going to miss you!"

"Me too!" Jenny's smile carried all the awakened desire and love she felt.

Then he was gone, leaving her staring after him. She closed the door softly when she heard the well-bred growl of the Porsche leaving. Then Jenny set about cleaning the apartment.

An essence of unreality clung to the morning. It was only because of long-standing habits and concentration that she was able to maintain a normal facade in front of Maggie. Half of her insisted on reliving every second of Daniel's passion. The other part was vainly fighting for the courage to face Edna Masters and the censure she expected for trying to enter society's magic circle.

Maggie's maternal pride and romantic nature surged to the fore at Jenny's announcement of the impending arrangements. She obviously shared none of Jenny's misgivings or doubts about the future. Her unswerving faith should have reassured Jenny, but strangely it didn't. Perversely, she felt deserted, unable to confide her deepest fears. Nervous, feeling like a defenseless creature caught in an alien world, Jenny sought refuge behind the tough-girl mask of her unwanted childhood—a defense that had been discarded years before but never forgotten.

It was this Jenny—cool, slightly flippant—who greeted the Masters matriarch in Azalea Hill's elegant drawing room. The impersonal accord that had characterized all of Jenny's dealings with the elder woman grew progressively distant, almost formal, as the afternoon wore on.

Entering her own apartment, Jenny tossed her navy blazer and white leather handbag at the chair near the door. "What a first-class witch I am," Jenny muttered in self-disgust. She kicked off her navy strapped sandals with an abrupt gesture. "After all these years, I had honestly thought I had outgrown my porcupine tendencies. What a fool!" Her short laugh was harsh in the silence of the empty room.

She had gotten exactly what she had expected and, she freely admitted, what she deserved. Edna Masters had been reserved but certainly not disapproving. She had been graciousness itself during their talk about the impending marriage and the party, even suggesting Jenny call her by her first name.

The party! If she could only call back those smart-mouth words of hers when Edna had offered to give her her dressmaker's name. At the time she had believed it was a not so subtly veiled dig at her less than affluent background.

Jenny's expression revealed her distaste at the memory of her snappy refusal. "That won't be necessary. Maggie, my assistant, is all the help I could possibly need."

It hadn't taken the quickly masked surprise and puzzlement to tell her how unforgivably rude and unnecessary her comment had been. Yet, even knowing that, she couldn't stop herself. It was as though all the pain and rejection had come bubbling up in her. It had taken the memory of Daniel and how much he meant to her to keep her civil.

It was as they were completing the tour in Daniel's wing of the house that her control broke once again.

Staring straight ahead, Jenny replayed the final scene in her mind. She could see the mellowed, old-world elegance of the robin's egg blue and white sitting room as clearly as her own living room. She could hear the silvery tones of her hostess's cultured voice.

"You will probably find this much more restful than the larger salon in the main house. When one isn't accustomed to those huge high ceilings, cozy places like this can be a haven." Edna smiled faintly. "I know I rarely have an opportunity to use my own retreat, but when I do I find it very relaxing."

Reading sarcasm where there was none, Jenny had not guarded her tongue. "No, I think I have a real affinity for the openness of these old rooms. It must come from being crammed into a dormitory with a lot of other kids," she had denied in quick defense.

It was then Jenny got a true picture of herself and her behavior. But it was too late to apologize. The damage was done. Edna the future mother-in-law became Mrs. Masters the society matriarch right before her eyes. In minutes, Jenny found herself politely shown the door.

Now what did she do? she wondered defeatedly,

slumping into a chair without regard for the white linen dress she had chosen to wear to Azalea Hill. What was she going to tell Daniel? How could she possibly explain away the seemingly deliberate antagonizing of his mother? Her mind boggled at the prospect.

Glancing at her watch, she saw it was late, almost suppertime. She never felt less like eating in her life. Before the evening was over, Daniel was going to call. Dear heaven, what would she say? This was one time she wished she weren't so blasted truthful.

Jenny had a good three hours to agonize over her behavior before the phone finally rang. The sound of Daniel's velvet drawl in her ears was warm and reassuring in the morass of her mental turmoil. Please let him understand, she prayed, gripping the receiver so tightly her knuckles shone white with tension. Once again she had failed in her belief in her own worth and in doing so, she had failed Daniel as well.

"How did your meeting with my mother go?" Daniel asked.

Closing her mind against the teasing gentleness in Daniel's question, Jenny steeled herself to tell him everything. She wished she could face him in person, yet she dared not take the chance of waiting for his return. She couldn't bear the thought of him finding out from someone else.

"Daniel," she began. Unknowingly, his name carried all the longing she felt for him and all her own unhappiness.

"Hey, what's wrong. I've only been gone for a few hours," Daniel chided her, misunderstanding the reason for the forlorn note in her voice.

"You may not ever want to speak to me again, let alone marry me," Jenny blurted, too miserable to waste time with careful words. "I've just spent the entire afternoon making your mother hate me." Jenny caught back a sob as she heard the telltale silence in her ear. She blinked to dispel the mist of tears blinding her. Silver droplets clung to the sable lashes like tiny diamonds.

"Jenny, are you crying?"

Jenny shook her head in answer to the stern voice.

"Jenny?" Sharper now, Daniel demanded a reply.

"No!" A treacherous wobble gave lie to her denial.

"Damn it, I'm coming home. What the devil did my mother say to you to get you in this state?" Daniel raged in frustration. He knew his mother was capable of being very polite and aloof if she chose, something that was bound to hurt Jenny with her hypersensitivity. He had been so sure Edna would not pull an act like that. He knew how much she admired and respected Jenny as a person.

Jenny was appalled. What had she done? "She didn't do anything, Daniel. It was me," Jenny hurried to explain, ignoring the grammatical inaccuracy. "I was so nervous, so stupidly defensive, I antagonized your mother. She was trying to be nice and I wouldn't let her. She even took me on a tour of her own wing, the whole house, in fact—"

"Damn the house," Daniel interrupted. "I couldn't care less about a pile of bricks and stone. It's you I'm concerned about." He paused, taking a deep breath before continuing in a quieter tone. "Now, if I understand you right, you're saying you pulled one of those prickly cactus stunts you used on your prospective foster parents when you were a kid."

"I'm afraid I did," Jenny agreed in a small voice. Relief at his calm attitude coursed through her. He didn't condemn her as she half feared. At least not yet.

175

"I never should have expected you to face her alone. I've rushed you into this situation and then left you to fend for yourself."

The weary acceptance of the blame for the afternoon's fiasco brought a sharp denial to Jenny's lips. "No, it's not your fault. It's mine. I should have acted like the adult I'm supposed to be, not the child I was." She was crying in earnest now, tears streaming down her face. First Daniel had blamed his mother, now himself. But not her, the one solely responsible. Was this a foretaste of their marriage? The pain, the disappointment. She couldn't do this to him. She loved him too much.

Dragging up every ounce of courage, every bit of willpower, Jenny tried to stem the rising tide of despair. No! She would not be a sniffling child any longer. This was the absolute last time Daniel was ever going to hear or think the word insecurity again. She was fighting for the love that gave her life meaning. She would not fail him again. Daniel's voice in her ear finally penetrated her thoughts.

". . . leave now, I should be back in Knoxville about ten. Reynolds—"

"No, I don't want you to come home because of this," Jenny interrupted firmly. "I am acting like a baby and we both know it. You were right in what you said before you left. I only wish I had fully realized it before I saw your mother. This is my problem and I must deal with it. And I will."

Jenny could hear Daniel's surprised reaction at her determined tone in the short silence that followed.

"Are you sure?" Relief mingled with concern in the brief question.

Jenny smiled, the dampness on her cheeks seeming out of place with the fierce love shining in her eyes. "As sure as I am that I'm going to marry you a week from Saturday," she vowed. It was her turn for reassurance.

Deep male laughter traveled the distance separating them, inviting Jenny's response.

"That just earned you a surprise from the big city," Daniel promised in a seductive growl with deliberately intimate undertones.

"As long as it's you," Jenny whispered in husky retaliation.

Saturday morning dawned bright and clear, a picture-perfect spring day. Jenny threw back the bedclothes and padded to her window to greet the sun. The ice blue sky feathered with snowy wisps of clouds promised a lovely balmy night for her engagement party.

Engagement! One more week and she would be Mrs. Daniel Masters! As she went to her closet to choose her clothes for the morning, she paused to admire the two plastic-wrapped creations she had chosen for the special days in her future.

The first was a pale lavender garden party gown in sheerest chiffon. The shirred neckline was the epitome of old southern elegance with its deep ruffle worn pulled off both shoulders. It was a gracefully sensual dress, appealing to the basic femininity of woman and the protective ardor of man. There was a slender purple velvet ribbon to wear around her neck that matched the velvet band around the deeply flounced hem.

The second gown was her wedding dress. Where the first had been a statement of demure gentleness, the second was the gift of a woman in love to her man. Rich cream silk and fine Irish lace combined to create an illusion of fire and passion. The sleeveless bodice was a plunging V filmed with lace over silk to just below the breasts. The skirt flowed softly to the floor in a smooth sweep of unadorned silk. Her veil was a fine mist of matching lace whispering to her shoulders. For a long moment, Jenny stood lost in a dream, imagining Daniel's face when he saw it.

The chime of her mantel clock brought an end to her musings, reminding her how late it was. She still had to dress, open the shop and make up that buffet centerpiece of lavender mums and white roses Edna had suggested for the party. If she didn't hurry, she wasn't going to be ready when Daniel arrived to take her out to Azalea Hill for the weekend. Not that her tardy appearance would be any great surprise to her fiancé. She hadn't been on time once since he returned from Atlanta.

With the wedding so close, there had been too much to do. First, and most important, had been making her apologies and explanations to her future mother-in-law. The meeting had gone surprisingly well, and while Jenny couldn't honestly say Edna welcomed her with open arms, she had been more than generous in her understanding. Knowing the older woman was prepared to meet her halfway in her efforts to become a wife whom Daniel could be proud of set the seal on the rest of the week.

It was a hectic time, yet she accomplished everything in the space allotted before the wedding. The dresses had been shopped for, her replacement had been interviewed, hired and trained. And of course time had been found for seeing Daniel—seeing being the operative word.

Except for one glorious uninhibited night the day he came back, she had been so tired from all her racing around, Daniel had left her early to rest. Daniel too was inundated with work, making even a hurried lunch an impossibility. The strain of both their hectic schedules and their reduced lovemaking was telling on them. Daniel's joke about counting the days was becoming increasingly apt. Thank heaven, it would all be over soon. Three weeks in the Bahamas alone with Daniel sounded more enticing by the hour. No phones, no worries, no people needing answers, no orders . . .

The promise of white sand beaches and Daniel at her side carried Jenny through the morning. Ellen, her replacement, after an initially slow start, finally appeared to have found her stride. Between her and the ever-helpful Maggie, Jenny managed to finish early for once. Taking the bonus hour, Jenny decided to shower and change into something more feminine than her usual pants. Daniel had been so good to her about her rushed schedule, she felt like dressing up for him. After laying out a primrose cotton sundress on her bed and a matching short-sleeved bolero jacket, she headed for the bathroom.

She stepped out of the shower just as her doorbell pealed. She quickly whipped the bath sheet around her dripping curves, tucking the end firmly between her breasts. She reached the door just when the bell rang again.

"I'm early . . ." Daniel's voice trailed to a halt as his gaze hungrily devoured the slender, tousled woman in the doorway. Tiny droplets of water lay like a mantle of glistening crystals on her bare shoulders before trickling slowly down to the firm swells of satiny skin above the pale blue towel. His eyes darkened as he stepped forward, reaching for her.

"Daniel, I'm dripping wet," Jenny cried, trying— but not too hard—to elude his grasp. When his hands caught her waist, drawing her against him, she made one final protest. "I'm going to ruin your suit."

"Damn my clothes," he murmured, his lips fastening possessively on hers.

Jenny met his kiss halfway, just as eager for him as

he was for her. The days of abstinence had only increased their need for each other, she found. She burned with desire at his first touch. Her body melted against his in surrender and feminine demand. When he scooped her into his arms, she only clung tighter, burying her lips in the strong column of his neck. Hungry to feel his bare skin against hers, she tugged at his tie until it was free, then started on the shirt buttons she could reach. Before she could finish the job, Daniel lowered her to the bed, still cradling her against him.

No words were spoken. None were needed. Their bodies communicated their mutual need, desire and love. Clothes showered to the floor until bare masculine strength fused with flaming urgency to gleaming feminine softness. It was a mating at its most primitive absolute. The peak, when it came, rose like a tidal wave cresting with terrible power, then crashing through all barriers of time, space and thought. Twin cries of exquisite release echoed in the passionate storm.

"That was some greeting," Daniel murmured against Jenny's ear as they lay entwined in each other's arms. His hands traveled slowly down Jenny's body from her bare breasts to her thigh, and then back again. It was a caress of ownership, of a man to his woman.

Jenny responded in kind, reveling in the feel of his firm muscled flesh beneath her fingers. "You were a little early," she murmured with a passion-laden throb.

"How I am going to get any sleep with you across the hall I don't know," Daniel groaned, burying his lips in her hair.

"I thought it was nice of your mother to second your invitation to spend the weekend, after my stupid behavior."

"After the trouble you went to make amends, she could hardly do otherwise. Going all the way out to the Hill when you weren't sure of your welcome, and then being so honest with her about your reasons for reacting the way you did really impressed her." He paused to press a rewarding kiss against her lips. "Know what she told me?"

"No, what?"

Daniel pulled Jenny over on top of him so he could see her face. "She said she knew I had chosen well for the Masters clan. She had no fears for the future generations."

Misty gray eyes searched Daniel's lean face. "Did she, really?" Jenny asked, hardly daring to believe the comprehensive accolade.

Daniel's lips curved into a gentle smile, softening the angular planes with tenderness. "Those were her very words," he assured her. For a long moment neither moved, as the mental rapport they had always shared strengthened and deepened with Jenny's personal victory. It was the first step, Jenny vowed.

"Come on, woman," Daniel chided at last, tickling Jenny's ribs. "Get your lovely bottom out of this bed. We have a party to attend."

Standing in front of the mirror in the lavender guest room that evening, Jenny relived the afternoon. Although she couldn't honestly say she had felt totally at ease in the huge house as she and Edna had attended to the last-minute details of the party, she had managed to keep any doubts she had hidden. Daniel had stayed only long enough for lunch before disappearing to collect the various people flying in especially for the event.

The guest floor of the main house had quickly filled, spilling over into Edna's wing. Only Daniel's side remained untouched. Here she and Daniel were isolated from the rest of the manse. Much as she enjoyed meeting the new arrivals, Jenny was grateful for the privacy. She needed it to prepare herself for the night ahead. This party was her own personal proving ground. She wanted desperately to marry Daniel, but she wouldn't if she couldn't be the wife he deserved. She loved him too much to hurt him by not being someone he could have pride in. Winning his mother over had only been half the battle. Meeting his friends and not shaming him with her obvious ignorance was just as important. If she succeeded tonight, she knew her past would no longer have the power to drive her. She would be free.

"Daydreaming?"

Jenny started at the sound of Daniel's voice. His image appeared in the mirror behind her own reflection. She caught her breath at the elegance of his formal attire. His silver gray dinner jacket over a cream silk shirt blended perfectly with her lavender gown, while his charcoal slacks echoed the dark bands of purple about her neck and her hem.

"Not exactly," she denied, leaning her head back against his shoulder without turning around. His arms encircled her waist, making one reflection out of two. "I was just thinking how easy this afternoon had been." It wasn't exactly the truth, but Jenny felt justified in stretching it a little.

Daniel leaned forward to drop a kiss on each bare shoulder. "You smell delicious. Taste good, too," he whispered deeply.

Jenny's eyes darkened as she felt the familiar warmth of desire wash over her skin.

"None of that," Daniel teased, catching sight of the longing she made no effort to hide.

"You started it," she reminded him with a seductive laugh. She gave her bottom a provocative twitch, then giggled at his instant response as she moved away. "Tit for tat," she teased.

Daniel's smile showed his acceptance of the woman he had created. "Something tells me in the years to come, I'm going to regret not keeping you more firmly in line," he retorted. He followed her gently swaying figure to the door.

Daniel pulled the door closed behind her and took her arm. His gaze swept over her, remembering the feel of her against him. "I didn't know you could still do that," he drawled, flicking a finger at one blushing cheek.

"Well, I can," Jenny grumbled crossly, shooting him an irritated look. "I'm not in the habit of having a man undressing me with his eyes."

"I'd rather it was my hands." He laughed out loud at her annoyance.

He pushed open the door that separated his wing from the rest of the house. At least she had more color in her cheeks, he decided, as they descended the stairs to the main hallway. He knew she was anxious about the party. He sensed it even though she was hiding it well. For her sake, he wanted everything to go well. It was one of the reasons he had chosen to hold this gathering. He wanted to show her off to his friends, but most of all, Jenny would be able to see how well she could fit in if she gave herself a chance. He was doubly glad Lionel Rockland had refused his mother's invitation. His wealthy, blunt-speaking uncle was one of the men he most respected in his circle, and normally he would be delighted to have him come. But not tonight.

Jenny knew nothing of Daniel's thoughts as she

entered the room on his arm. Her initial nervousness had disappeared under Daniel's teasing, allowing her natural personality to blossom. With a smile curving her lips Jenny took her place in the receiving line.

Flanked by Daniel and his mother, she found it surprisingly easy to greet the steady stream of guests with the graceful aplomb the occasion demanded. The sincere compliments and the genuine warmth of those she met allayed any lingering doubts she had. The cream of Knoxville's society had accepted her in spite of her lack of background. True, there were a few raised eyebrows, but nothing like she had feared. For the first hour or so, Daniel hovered protectively at her side. But as her confidence grew, they separated, circulating among the hundred or so friends.

Jenny paused at the open terrace windows, momentarily alone. Around her, people were smiling and chatting, obviously enjoying the lavish hospitality. White-coated waiters, bearing silver trays of tidbits and iced champagne, moved among the colorful throng. Soft strains of violins from the hired orchestra drifted through the open doorway between the ballroom and main salon.

Jenny's gaze traveled slowly around the room until she found Daniel's tawny head above the crowd. She smiled when he looked up and caught her eye. She felt the desire in him as though he had reached across the distance and caressed her bare skin. His look said, "I love you, I desire you, and I want you in my arms."

She answered, "Here?"

His brow quirked eloquently while he flickered a glance to the ballroom. Jenny smiled her eagerness and began to move gracefully toward the open doorway. She nodded to Edna as she passed a small group of ladies where she was holding court.

She was even with the main door when she realized one guest, obviously a late-comer, stood surveying the gathering. In his late sixties, the man had the tall, lean look of Daniel without the clear aristocratic bone structure. He had a silver-white mane of hair above white, bushy brows, and his chiseled features were a perfect setting for the piercing blue eyes of the new arrival. He looked out of place, Jenny felt, going to greet him—a fellow sufferer in this affluent world.

Smiling, hoping to put him at ease, Jenny held out her hand. "Hello, I'm Jennifer, welcome to our home." Simple words, but they carried a wealth of sincerity and surprising self-assurance.

"*Your* home?" the man questioned gruffly, raising an eyebrow in unknowing imitation of her fiancé. "I thought only Daniel and his mother lived here."

"Right now they do," Jenny agreed, ignoring his bluntness. Hadn't she been just as outspoken when she felt nervous? "Daniel and I are getting married next week."

"Rather rushed, wasn't it?"

Jenny heard the speculative note in the short question and wondered at it. Who was this man? He had the look of Daniel, but certainly not the manners. Glancing around, she saw Daniel, a strange, almost protective look on his face, making his way toward them. "Well, Daniel wanted it sooner, but we both had some loose business ends to tie up before we felt we could take time off for a honeymoon."

"You don't mind playing second fiddle to his business interests?"

There was an odd gleam in the shrewd blue eyes that could have been teasing if the tone of his remark hadn't been so serious.

"I don't feel I'm second to anything," Jenny stated, keeping a smile on her face with an effort.

Bushy brows rose in surprise at her quick reply. "You're very understanding. I can see why Daniel speaks so highly of you," he responded, allowing a smile to soften the hard planes of his face. His eyes twinkled engagingly, dispelling the stern image he had projected.

"He does?" Jenny questioned, startled at the sudden change.

"Oh yes, my dear. Daniel bent my ear for over an hour in singing your praises." He leaned forward to place a paternal kiss on her cheek. "Welcome to the family, Jenny Brown. You may call me Lion."

Jenny smiled her thanks, too dazed to speak. Suddenly she knew who her guest was. Lionel J. Rockland, financial wizard, political powerhouse, the terror of the southeast and the man behind most of the big legislative deals in Tennessee . . . and Daniel's uncle.

Daniel's arm around her waist came just in time to save her from going to the floor in a crumpled heap. "What have you been saying to Jenny, Lion?" Daniel demanded, feeling Jenny lean heavily against his side. He glanced at her stunned face before frowning angrily at his blunt-spoken uncle. His arm tightened protectively around her slender curves.

Hearing the fierce note edging Daniel's voice, Jenny collected her scattered senses. "He was just teasing me, Daniel," she said when the other man made no effort to answer. "I'm afraid I had no idea who you were," she added, glancing at Lion apologetically.

He grinned. "I could tell. You'll have to forgive an old man his idiosyncrasies. I wanted to see if Daniel had chosen well." He chuckled as Daniel glared at him. "He did." He glanced beyond the couple facing him. "Ah, I see my sister heading this way, no doubt intending to lend her support. I think I'll go talk to that stunning blonde I see by the windows." With a nod, he strolled off toward his goal, leaving Daniel and Jennifer staring after him.

"Crazy old man," Daniel grunted, affection and reluctant admiration taking the sting from his words. "I was hoping he wouldn't come until you had a chance to become more accustomed to my life."

Jenny smiled, pure happiness lighting her face. She had done it! She had met her fears and conquered them. Lionel Rockland was feared everywhere for his ability to cut anyone who didn't come up to his standards. She had met her worst possible critic and won. Now she could come to Daniel untainted by her past.

"I'm glad he did. Besides, I like him."

Daniel leaned down to brush her lips with his. "You do, do you?" he growled.

She nodded, gray eyes shimmering with happiness.

Daniel's eyes flickered briefly in the direction of his uncle before returning to Jenny's animated face. "As long as you don't like him too much. But enough about him, let's talk about us—I want to hold you now, Jenny." He guided her toward the ballroom, not releasing his hold on her waist even when they stepped onto the glass smooth floor.

Jenny floated into Daniel's arms and smiled into his indigo eyes. The smoke-gray depths of her own reflected the same burning desire in his.

"Do you believe me now, Jenny Brown? Do you see how little your background matters?" he whispered against her ear. His laugh was a husky rumble of amusement. "You even tamed the Lion." He tightened his embrace, drawing Jenny closer until not even a breath of air separated them. "You're finally truly mine. Admit it."

"I love you, Daniel. You're all I'll ever need,"

187

Jenny purred in a deep throb of heightened emotion, oblivious to the people around them.

Daniel understood her as no one else did. This one man was the family she longed for, the name she never really had, and the love she had never known. She had finally won her heart's desire. She had come home at last.

Silhouette Desire
15-Day Trial Offer
A new romance series
that explores
contemporary relationships
in exciting detail

Six Silhouette Desire romances, free for 15 days!
We'll send you six new Silhouette Desire romances
to look over for 15 days, absolutely free! If you decide
not to keep the books, return them and owe nothing.

Six books a month, free home delivery. If you like
Silhouette Desire romances as much as we think you
will, keep them and return your payment with the
invoice. Then we will send you six new books every
month to preview, just as soon as they are published.
You pay only for the books you decide to keep, and
you never pay postage and handling.

YOU'LL BE SWEPT AWAY WITH SILHOUETTE DESIRE

$1.75 each

1 ☐ CORPORATE AFFAIR
James

2 ☐ LOVE'S SILVER WEB
Monet

3 ☐ WISE FOLLY
Clay

4 ☐ KISS AND TELL
Carey

5 ☐ WHEN LAST WE
LOVED
Baker

6 ☐ A FRENCHMAN'S KISS
Mallory

7 ☐ NOT EVEN FOR LOVE
St. Claire

8 ☐ MAKE NO PROMISES
Dee

9 ☐ MOMENT IN TIME
Simms

10 ☐ WHENEVER I LOVE
YOU Smith

$1.95 each

11 ☐ VELVET TOUCH
James

12 ☐ THE COWBOY AND
THE LADY Palmer

13 ☐ COME BACK, MY
LOVE Wallace

14 ☐ BLANKET OF STARS
Valley

15 ☐ SWEET BONDAGE
Vernon

16 ☐ DREAM COME TRUE
Major

17 ☐ OF PASSION BORN
Simms

18 ☐ SECOND HARVEST
Ross

19 ☐ LOVER IN PURSUIT
James

20 ☐ KING OF DIAMONDS
Allison

21 ☐ LOVE IN THE CHINA
SEA Baker

22 ☐ BITTERSWEET IN
BERN Durant

23 ☐ CONSTANT
STRANGER Sunshine

24 ☐ SHARED MOMENTS
Baxter

25 ☐ RENAISSANCE MAN
James

26 ☐ SEPTEMBER
MORNING Palmer

27 ☐ ON WINGS OF NIGHT
Conrad

28 ☐ PASSIONATE
JOURNEY Lovan

29 ☐ ENCHANTED DESERT
Michelle

30 ☐ PAST FORGETTING
Lind

31 ☐ RECKLESS PASSION
James

32 ☐ YESTERDAY'S
DREAMS Clay

33 ☐ PROMISE ME
TOMORROW Powers

34 ☐ SNOW SPIRIT
Milan

35 ☐ MEANT TO BE
Major

36 ☐ FIRES OF MEMORY
Summers

37 ☐ PRICE OF SURRENDER
James

38 ☐ SWEET SERENITY
Douglass

39 ☐ SHADOW OF
BETRAYAL Monet

40 ☐ GENTLE CONQUEST
Mallory

41 ☐ SEDUCTION BY
DESIGN St. Claire

42 ☐ ASK ME NO SECRETS
Stewart

43 ☐ A WILD, SWEET
MAGIC Simms

44 ☐ HEART OVER MIND
West

45 ☐ EXPERIMENT IN LOVE
Clay

46 ☐ HER GOLDEN EYES
Chance

47 ☐ SILVER PROMISES
Michelle

48 ☐ DREAM OF THE WEST
Powers

49 ☐ AFFAIR OF HONOR
James

Silhouette Desire

50 ☐ FRIENDS AND LOVERS Palmer	64 ☐ SONATINA Milan	79 ☐ SO SWEET A MADNESS Simms
51 ☐ SHADOW OF THE MOUNTAIN Lind	65 ☐ RECKLESS VENTURE Allison	80 ☐ FIRE AND ICE Palmer
52 ☐ EMBERS OF THE SUN Morgan	66 ☐ THE FIERCE GENTLENESS Langtry	81 ☐ OPENING BID Kennedy
53 ☐ WINTER LADY Joyce	67 ☐ GAMEMASTER James	82 ☐ SUMMER SONG Clay
54 ☐ IF EVER YOU NEED ME Fulford	68 ☐ SHADOW OF YESTERDAY Browning	83 ☐ HOME AT LAST Chance
55 ☐ TO TAME THE HUNTER James	69 ☐ PASSION'S PORTRAIT Carey	84 ☐ IN A MOMENT'S TIME Powers
56 ☐ FLIP SIDE OF YESTERDAY Douglass	70 ☐ DINNER FOR TWO Victor	85 ☐ THE SILVER SNARE James
57 ☐ NO PLACE FOR A WOMAN Michelle	71 ☐ MAN OF THE HOUSE Joyce	86 ☐ NATIVE SEASON Malek
58 ☐ ONE NIGHT'S DECEPTION Mallory	72 ☐ NOBODY'S BABY Hart	87 ☐ RECIPE FOR LOVE Michelle
59 ☐ TIME STANDS STILL Powers	73 ☐ A KISS REMEMBERED St. Claire	88 ☐ WINGED VICTORY Trevor
60 ☐ BETWEEN THE LINES Dennis	74 ☐ BEYOND FANTASY Douglass	89 ☐ TIME FOR TOMORROW Ross
61 ☐ ALL THE NIGHT LONG Simms	75 ☐ CHASE THE CLOUDS McKenna	90 ☐ WILD FLIGHT Roszel
62 ☐ PASSIONATE SILENCE Monet	76 ☐ STORMY SERENADE Michelle	
63 ☐ SHARE YOUR TOMORROWS Dee	77 ☐ SUMMER THUNDER Lowell	
	78 ☐ BLUEPRINT FOR RAPTURE Barber	

SILHOUETTE DESIRE, Department SD/6
1230 Avenue of the Americas
New York, NY 10020

Please send me the books I have checked above. I am enclosing $\rule{3cm}{0.4pt}$
(please add 50¢ to the cover postage and handling. NYS and NYC residents please add appropriate sales tax.) Send check or money order—no cash or C.O.D.'s please. Allow six weeks for delivery.

NAME

ADDRESS

CITY _____ STATE/ZIP

Get 6 new
Silhouette Special Editions
every month
for a 15–day FREE trial!

Free Home Delivery, Free Previews, Free Bonus Books.
Silhouette Special Editions are a new kind of romance
novel. These are big, powerful stories that will capture
your imagination. They're longer, with fully developed
characters and intricate plots that will hold you spell-
bound from the first page to the very last.

Each month we will send you six exciting *new*
Silhouette Special Editions, just as soon as they are published. If you enjoy them as much as we think you will,
pay the invoice enclosed with your shipment. **They're
delivered right to your door with never a charge for
postage or handling, and there's no obligation to buy
anything at any time.** To start receiving Silhouette Special
Editions regularly, mail the coupon below today.

Silhouette Special Edition